Lemon Drizzle and Murder

Holly Holmes Cozy Culinary Mystery - book 7

K.E. O'Connor

K.E. O'Connor Books

While every precaution has been taken in the preparation of this book, the publisher assumes no responsibility for errors or omissions, or for damages resulting from the use of the information contained herein.

All rights reserved.

No portion of this book may be reproduced in any form without written permission from the publisher or author, except as permitted by U.S. copyright law.

LEMON DRIZZLE AND MURDER

Copyright © 2021 K.E. O'Connor.

ISBN: 978-1-9163573-6-5

Written by K.E. O'Connor

Edited by Amy Hart

Cover design by Stunning Book Covers

Beta read by my wonderful early review team. You're all amazing.

Chapter 1

"Let's see if the restorers need feeding." I balanced a full tray of leftover cakes and sandwiches in my hands, excitement running through me at the thought of spending an evening immersed in a rare historical discovery.

Meatball, my adorable corgi cross, bounced around my feet, keen to see what delicious food might be available for him.

"There's none for you. You're having dinner soon. Come on, let's take a look in the east turret and see how they're getting on."

Audley Castle was hosting a small team of expert restorers, who were working on a stunning renovation of a ceiling painting uncovered in the old gallery.

I'd put myself in charge of keeping them fed. But really, it was so I could watch their progress and marvel at their finds.

I'd only made it a dozen steps from the back door of the castle kitchen, when Campbell Milligan stepped into my path.

"Holly, what are you up to?" He arched an eyebrow.

"Jeez, give a girl a break. Why are you lurking in the shadows back here?"

"I never lurk. What are you doing with that cake?" He snagged a piece of lemon drizzle cake from the tray.

"Giving it to more deserving people than you. Hands off. I'm going to see how the restoration work is going."

Campbell shook his head as he walked along beside me. "That's a terrible idea. It's a death trap in the old gallery."

"What are you talking about?"

He grabbed the tray out of my hands. "Allow me. That looks heavy."

I narrowed my eyes at him. "So long as you don't eat any more."

"I may have one or two slices of cake. Call it my payment."

"So, the old gallery is a death trap?"

"I've been in there a few times since they started work. It's chaos. There are tools and equipment everywhere. They don't know what they're doing."

"The Duke and Duchess wouldn't allow just anyone into the castle. Herbert Fitzwilliam-Smithe is an expert in art restoration. He's been doing it for thirty-five years. He lectures at Oxford and Cambridge and goes all over the world showcasing his efforts to preserve fragile art."

Campbell snorted. "I forgot you were a history geek."

"There's nothing geeky about history. I can't wait to see how they've been getting on." The restoration crew had been in the east turret for eight days, painstakingly cleaning the ceiling art.

"There are dozens of paintings in the main castle. There's nothing exciting about this one," Campbell said.

"It's been hidden under layers of dirt for hundreds of years. The last time I went to take a look, they'd uncovered a piece of sky. And there were angels. It'll be stunning when it's finished."

He grunted. "Well, just be careful when you're staring at the ceiling. The stairs were wet when I checked on the security arrangements. They're using some cleaning technique that means everything gets soaked. I'm not sure about the guy who's in charge."

"Herbert's sweet. And he knows what he's talking about."

"Sweet's one word for him. The last time I spoke to him, he had his jacket on inside out and his shirt misbuttoned."

"He's eccentric. He's more interested in his work than looking smart. There's no harm in that."

Campbell reached for another piece of lemon drizzle cake.

I smacked the back of his hand. "That's not for you. Give me the tray if you can't control yourself." We reached the entrance to the east turret.

Meatball bounded in ahead, barking with excitement, the sound echoing off the stone walls.

Usually, neither of us were keen to go into the east turret, given its unusual cold spots and strange ghostly whispers, but this time was different.

"Don't say I didn't warn you." Campbell grabbed a piece of cake and strode away before I had a chance to tell him off.

I shook my head, then walked inside. There was a spiral staircase in the middle of the turret that led to Lady Philippa Audley's private rooms, and three large open plan rooms on the lower level.

The old gallery was what interested me the most. A leak on one wall six months ago had exposed a piece of the hidden art. It had been examined, and the family decided to have the whole room updated and restored to welcome even more visitors to the castle.

I dodged around puddles on the floor and several tools and headed into the room.

There was a huge row of scaffolding set along one wall that reached up to the ceiling. There was a woman working up the top in one corner. I recognized her as Sara Silverman, one of the assistant restorers.

"Holly! You're an angel. You come bearing gifts again." Herbert Fitzwilliam-Smithe wandered over, pushing his small, round glasses up his long nose. He definitely fitted the mold of an eccentric historian, with his white hair pulled back in a ponytail and mismatching clothes. But I'd enjoyed the chats we'd had. He knew everything about this particular historical period and was passionate about restoration work.

"I don't want to see you go hungry. And of course, I'd love to have a peek at what you're doing. How's it going?" I nudged aside more tools with the tray and set it down on the painting table.

"We've had an excellent day. We've been using the water washing technique to remove the crusted-on dirt. It means we get a better look at what we're working with. Watch out for the puddles, though. We had a problem with the hose. Justin lost control and sent water everywhere. I'm grateful the walls are made of stone, so they'll dry out. Come take a look."

"Herbert, where's the report I asked you for?" A petite brunette with a cut-glass British accent marched over. She glared at me. "Oh, you're here again."

"Hi, Bluebell. I wanted to see how you've been getting on. Would you like some cake? I've brought lemon drizzle," I said as sweetly as I could. Every time I met Bluebell Brewster, she looked at me as if I was something unpleasant she'd found on the sole of her shoe.

She peered down her nose at me. "Herbert, the report? I have to submit it to Greta. We're already two days late getting the information she needs."

Herbert smoothed a hand over his unruly hair and his cheeks flushed bright red. "Of course. I got side-tracked by an incredible discovery. Apparently, the layout—"

"I'm not interested in layouts. Focus on your task. You have to provide the reports to show we're making progress. We can't waste our funder's time, or they'll withdraw their support."

"They won't stop funding us." Herbert smiled and nodded. "This is too important."

"They will if we don't tell them what we're doing," Bluebell said.

His warm smile faded. "Of course. I'll get right onto the report."

"You haven't even started it?" Bluebell scowled at him. She was at least ten years younger than Herbert but was definitely the boss around here. "Greta will be here soon. She won't be happy to hear about this."

"Oh! Don't tell Greta. She doesn't understand our work." Herbert flapped a hand in the air.

"She understands finances, which is why she's overseeing this project. If you keep messing up, she'll get rid of you. I don't care how many PhDs you have, or how many years lecturing to wide-eyed students. We work in the private sector now. That's where the money is."

"I think Herbert and his assistants are doing a great job," I said. "If you brought your funder to see the progress, they'd be interested. They wouldn't want to stop this from being finished. It'll be so beautiful when it's done."

Bluebell glanced at me. "What's your specialty again?"

"Holly studied history at university," Herbert said. "She's got an interest in our work."

"And yet she works in the castle kitchens," Bluebell said. "Isn't it time you got back to your baking and stopped distracting my work crew?"

Meatball raced over and bounded around Bluebell, leaping up and pressing his damp paws onto her pristine pale gray pants.

"Ugh! What's he doing here?" Bluebell stepped back into a pool of water and scowled. "For goodness sake. Herbert, clean this place up and get on with the report. If I have to ask you again, I'll rethink the management structure and send you back to the university." She turned and stalked away.

"Oh dear," Herbert said with a sigh. "Bluebell doesn't seem happy with me. She's a demanding woman."

From the adoring look in his eyes, that wasn't all he thought about Bluebell.

"Is that cake?" Justin Banderas bounded over on long, thin legs. He gave me a huge smile as he shoved his scruffy, shoulder-length brown hair out of his eyes. "I'm starving. Thanks, Holly." He set to work on a huge slice of lemon drizzle cake, his free hand reaching for a sandwich.

"You're welcome. It would have only gone to waste. We can't keep things like this overnight because it doesn't stay fresh." I grinned as Justin continued to shovel in food. He definitely needed filling out. He was rake thin. And from the threadbare appearance of his clothes, I got the impression he didn't earn much. I doubted assistant restorers ever got rich. They did this work because they were passionate about it.

"Sara, come down. Holly's brought us food," Justin yelled, covering his mouth to avoid splattering everyone with crumbs.

Sara turned and waved a hand in acknowledgement. She unclipped the safety harness that attached her to the scaffolding, then climbed down a ladder. She walked over, wiping her hands on a cloth before tucking it into the waistband of her pants.

"Great. I've been working up on that scaffold all day. I'm famished." Sara Silverman was the opposite of Justin. She was short and plump, with round cheeks that were speckled with freckles and shoulder-length red hair.

"How's the restoration work going?" I said.

"Come take a look," Sara said. "I'm proud of what we've uncovered."

I followed her to the bottom of the scaffold with Herbert and Justin.

"Justin, switch on the spotlight. The light's fading." Sara grinned at me. "Or you can shin up the ladder and take a look if you're feeling adventurous."

"Don't go up there." Justin wheeled over a large spotlight and aimed it at the ceiling. "It's horribly high. You'll never get me up to the top."

"It's not so bad when you get used to it," Sara said. "You're missing out on all the fun."

He shuddered. "I have no head for heights."

Sara squeezed his arm. "Don't worry. I'll do all the high work. Take a look at that, Holly. We think this could be an original painting from Witkor Alderman."

"I've heard of that name," I said.

"He was famous a few hundred years ago. He was everyone's go-to guy when it came to creating elaborate works of art in hard to reach places. He was like the Banksy of medieval times. There are numerous cracks in the original plaster work, but this will clean up well," Sara said.

Justin munched on a sandwich as he adjusted the spotlight and beamed it on the painting. There were dull splashes of blue and white, along with what may have been an arm.

"Holly! There you are."

I turned just as Princess Alice Audley shrieked, skidded in a puddle of water, and landed flat on her back.

Herbert gasped, and Justin dropped his sandwich.

I raced over with Sara to help Alice up.

"Are you okay?" I grabbed her arm.

"Oh! Princess Alice, I'm so sorry." Herbert rushed over. "I should have signs up. Bluebell's been telling me to put up the hazard markings, but I've been distracted by some fascinating research about Audley Castle."

Alice accepted his hand and pulled herself upright before brushing down the back of her soaked pink dress. "Don't worry about me. I never look where I'm going. I'm almost as bad as my dopey brother. Holly, I was hoping we could have dinner together tonight."

"Oh, sure. I'm free. I was just having a look at the restoration work."

"Campbell told me you were here." She glanced around. "He also told me to be careful. Don't mention my little trip to him. He'll only tell me that he told me so."

"Our secret's safe," I said.

"Princess Alice, I'm so glad you're here," Herbert said. "I've been reading about the legendary gold chalice that inspired the painting on the ceiling. I believe that when the work is finished, we'll find a depiction of the chalice. Wouldn't that be remarkable?"

"You're talking about the Audley goblet?" she asked.

"That's it. Some people call it a goblet, some call it a chalice."

"Or a bowl," Justin said as he took more cake. "No one's sure what it actually looks like."

Herbert nodded. "There are all sorts of fascinating theories about its origins, and where it's been hidden."

"I've never heard about this chalice," I said.

"It's a myth," Alice said.

"There's often truth in myths," Herbert said.

"Tell that to the Loch Ness monster." I grinned at him.

"She was a real beast," Herbert said. "Although monster hunting isn't my specialty, I have a colleague at Exeter University who has visual proof of the creature."

"I'd love to see that," Alice said. "Holly, we should arrange a visit. And we can take Herbert's friend with us so he can point out the best viewing spots."

Herbert chuckled. "Ah, I don't think you'll find Nessie alive any longer. She'd be hundreds of years old. But I can have him send you some photos."

"Oh, that's not such fun," Alice said.

"What about the Audley chalice?" I said. "You said that no one's ever seen it."

"Not for hundreds of years," Herbert said. "It's believed to be made of solid gold and embedded with rubies and sapphires."

Justin whistled. "That would be worth a lot of money."

"A fortune," Herbert said. "There'd be a huge amount of interest in the historical community if it was ever found."

"It's not real," Alice said. "Granny sometimes mentions the goblet. She's convinced it's hidden somewhere in the castle. I've looked everywhere. I'd know if there was a priceless chalice hiding anywhere."

"Imagine what you could do with all the money if you sold it," I said.

"Build another castle," Alice said. "One with fewer drafts and walls that don't leak."

"I'd have a new wing of the university built and named after me," Herbert said. "The Herbert Fitzwilliam-Smithe lecture hall. That has a ring to it."

"I'd pay off my student debts," Justin said. "And move out of my dingy apartment."

"Same here," Sara said. "Then go on a luxury cruise."

"You could do a lot more with the money than that," Alice said. "But as I keep saying, it's not real."

"I hope we do find a depiction of it once we've removed the dirt on the painting," Herbert said.

Alice wandered about, flipping up the waterproof sheeting covering the statues around the old gallery.

She uncovered one and patted its head. "My great-grandfather will be looking on with interest. But you'll be disappointed if you're hoping to find the goblet."

"A painting of it would be enough for me," Herbert said. "It would prove its existence."

"Or it would prove someone had an active imagination a few hundred years ago," Alice said. "Come on, Holly. I'm starving. Let's go have dinner. I've ordered a delicious treat from the kitchen."

I shook my head. "Chef Heston won't be pleased to know he's providing my dinner tonight."

"He'll get over it. He always does. His bark is worse than his bite."

We said goodbye to Herbert, Sara, and Justin, and headed out of the old gallery.

Meatball raced after us, bouncing around me.

"I know. It's dinner time," I said.

"I haven't left Meatball out," Alice said. "I ordered him a special bowl of braised beef and vegetables."

I groaned. "Chef Heston will kill me. Now, he's feeding Meatball, too."

"He loves cooking. And I didn't say the food was for you and Meatball."

"He'll know. He always does." I dodged around Meatball as he continued to bounce in front of me. My foot hit a piece of pipe sticking out from under a cloth.

I grabbed my toe and yelped.

"What's the matter?" Alice said.

"My toe! I just whacked it." I hopped on one foot, wriggling my sore toe. My foot slipped from under me on the wet stone.

Meatball dodged around me, and I pitched over, smacking my head on the damp wall.

Everything went fuzzy for a few seconds, then an icy touch drifted across my cheek.

I twisted my head, but there was no one beside me.

I rolled over, blinked several times, and came face-to-face with a skull.

Chapter 2

"Holly! Can you hear me? Are you dead?" Alice loomed into view, her face pale. She grabbed my shoulder and shook me.

"Don't worry about me. There's a skull under that cloth." I pointed a shaking hand at the morbid discovery.

"A skull!" Alice strode over and pulled up the cloth. "Oh! That's Great-Uncle Theobald. What's he doing here?" She grabbed the skull and hauled it out.

"Um, you know this skull?" I rubbed my sore head and toe.

Herbert appeared with Sara and Justin.

"My dear girl. I'm so sorry," Herbert said. "I've been meaning to get the water dried out, but I've been distracted."

"I'm good. But we found a skull." I pointed at Alice, who was whispering to the skull.

"We're related. Say hello to my great-uncle Theobald." Alice turned the skull from side to side.

I shuffled upright and looked around. "Was someone else here a second ago? I'm sure they touched me just after I fell."

"Other than me, no." Alice turned to me. "You scared me when you fell over. Are you hurt?"

I touched my cheek, which still felt icy. "Nothing's broken. Are you sure no one was looking at me?"

She crouched next to me, the skull under her arm. "Positive. Did you hit your head?"

I touched my forehead. "Yes, but not hard."

"I'd better call for an ambulance," Alice said.

"I'm okay, I think. There's no need for an ambulance."

"Let's get you up. Justin, help me get Holly on her feet," Herbert said.

"Of course." Justin hurried to my side, and between the two of them, they got me standing.

The second my left foot hit the ground, a sharp, throbbing pain shot up into my calf.

"You don't look so good," Sara said. "You've gone pale. You should sit down."

"Maybe we should call for an ambulance," Alice said.

"No, it's my ankle. I must have twisted it," I said. "I'll be fine. There's no need to go to the hospital."

"I'll get the castle doctor to visit you," Alice said. "I'll make the call now."

Herbert and Justin helped me to a seat, and I settled in it, grimacing as my damp clothing stuck to my skin.

I carefully twisted my ankle and instantly regretted it as the pain flared again.

"Is there anything I can do for you?" Herbert said. "I feel terribly guilty. Bluebell is always telling me that I'm messy."

"Who's talking about me?" Bluebell strode into the room. She glared at me. "What's the matter with her?"

"I tripped over," I said.

Bluebell rolled her eyes. "Idiot. We have expensive equipment in here. You could have damaged something."

"Then you need to be more careful about keeping your expensive tools tidied away so people don't have accidents," I said.

Bluebell pursed her lips. "You're not even supposed to be here. We don't need a kitchen assistant blundering around and damaging things."

"Holly's been hurt. And she's been looking after us ever since we arrived," Sara said.

"You can keep quiet if you want to keep your apprenticeship." Bluebell jabbed a finger at Sara, then strode away.

Sara glared after her before turning back to me. "Ignore her. Greta's hassling her to get results, so she takes it out on us."

"It's my fault. I wasn't looking where I was going. And Meatball was getting under my feet," I said.

Meatball crept over on his belly, his tail down. He gently licked the back of my hand.

I stroked his head. "You're fine. I don't blame you, either."

Alice walked over. "It's all sorted. The doctor will meet you at your apartment. And I've arranged for Campbell to help you get back there."

I grimaced. "Can't you find someone else?"

"Campbell may as well put his muscles to good use."

I narrowed my eyes at her. "Alice, what have you told him to do?"

"I've ordered him to carry you back to the apartment."

I dropped my head into my hands. This was so humiliating. "I'll be able to walk back if I have time to rest."

"Absolutely not. He'll be here any minute," Alice said.

Justin passed me a piece of lemon drizzle cake. "Have this. Sugar's supposed to be good for shock, isn't it?"

"Thanks." I nibbled on the cake. The intense lemon sharp sweetness did make me feel better, although my ankle continued to throb.

Campbell strode into the gallery a few minutes later. The tight expression on his face showed exactly what he thought about the order Alice had given him.

He walked over, and his gaze ran over me. "What have you done this time, Holmes?"

"She nearly died," Alice said. "And she found Great-Uncle Theobald hiding from us."

Campbell glanced at the skull. "Very good, Princess. Are you ready to go?" he asked me.

"Yes. I was nowhere near death, but I wouldn't mind getting back to my apartment," I said.

"We need to get you in dry clothing, get that foot up, and then get you fed," Alice said. "Oh, dinner! Chef Heston will be wondering where I am. I'll tell him to bring it to your apartment. We can eat there. I'll get extra for your gran. I'll meet you back there." Alice dashed away before I had a chance to stop her.

"Dining with the nobility again?" Campbell said. "People will talk."

"Those people can mind their own business," I said. I huffed out a breath. "So, how do you want to do this?"

A smile flickered across Campbell's face. "I could give you a fireman's lift."

I looked up at him. It was impossible to tell if he was joking. "I'd rather walk back than have you hoist me over your shoulder like a sack of potatoes."

"You shouldn't walk on that ankle. You'll do more damage. Let this man carry you. He looks strong." Sara risked her life by giving Campbell's bicep a squeeze. "Oh, my! Yes, I'm sure he can carry you."

"Sara!" Justin hissed. "Don't be rude."

"I was just checking he was up to the job." Sara's cheeks flushed, and she stepped back.

"Let's do this." Campbell scooped me into his arms, one hand going under my knees and the other going around my back.

I shot into the air and grabbed hold of his shoulders.

"Feel better soon." Herbert hurried along beside us as Campbell strode away. "And come back any time. I hope this hasn't put you off of seeing our work."

"I'll definitely be back." I waved the others goodbye as we left the old gallery.

Campbell marched along the pathway, heading toward my apartment. "I did warn you that place was a death trap. What were you playing at?"

"I was an idiot. I wasn't looking where I was going."

"There'll be no running for you for a while. That ankle looks puffy."

There was a silver lining to every cloud. Running wasn't my favorite pastime. I only did it so I could get away with eating more cake.

As we reached my apartment, the castle doctor was pulling up in his car. He climbed out and raised his hand in greeting. "Perfect timing. How's the patient?"

"Heavy," Campbell said.

"You can put me down. I can walk the rest of the way if you're struggling."

Campbell ignored me and headed to the door. The doctor knocked on it, and Gran opened it a few seconds later.

Meatball dashed in and bounced around with Gran's Chihuahua, Saffron.

"What have we got here?" Gran said. "Holly, why are you in Campbell's arms?"

"She had a fall," Campbell said.

"You're hurt?" Gran stepped back to let everyone in. "What happened?"

I gave her a brief summary of my accident, while the doctor checked over my ankle, and Campbell loomed beside the couch.

"You're too nosy for your own good," Campbell said.

"A healthy curiosity isn't a bad thing." Gran shot him a glare, then sighed. "I should thank you for bringing my granddaughter back to me in one piece. Even if that piece is puffy and sore looking."

Campbell simply nodded.

"You'll be fine." The doctor gently patted my knee. "There's no break, but it is badly sprained. You'll need to rest the foot for at least three days. Try not to put any weight on it. And keep it elevated. That'll help bring down the swelling. Apply ice if it gets painful, and you'll be fine in a couple of weeks."

"Two weeks. I have a job to do."

"Not for the next few days, you don't. I advise complete rest." The doctor stood and packed away his medical bag. "Any problems, you know where to find me."

"Thank you, Doctor." Gran led him to the door, and he left.

She'd just walked away, when there was a loud knock on the door. She returned and opened it.

I peered around the corner to see who it was.

Lord Rupert Audley stood outside, a pile of books in his hands and a huge box of chocolates balanced on top of them. "I heard Holly was injured. I came to see how she was."

"Isn't that sweet." Gran smiled at him indulgently. "Come in. Holly will be thrilled to see you."

"Thank you." He hurried into the living room. "There you are. Alice told me what happened. How's your head?"

"You didn't mention a problem with your head to the doctor," Campbell said.

I waved away his comment. "It was nothing. I didn't pass out, I just bumped it on my way down. It's my ankle I'm most worried about."

Campbell knelt beside me and raised a finger. "Follow this with your eyes."

"You're being ridiculous," I said.

"I'm never ridiculous. Do it. Head injuries aren't something to joke about."

"I don't need you playing doctor with me."

"Maybe you should. Campbell knows his stuff. He's had military training," Rupert said. "Please, for me."

I groaned. "Fine. Do your weird tests. But you're wasting your time."

"Follow my finger," Campbell said. "Good. Do you have blurry vision or sickness?"

"No. I feel amazing."

"How many fingers am I holding up?"

"Enough! I can see just fine. You're overreacting."

"Are you sure there's nothing else?" Campbell's eyes narrowed.

"Positive. Don't you have people to guard?"

Campbell grunted. "I do need to get back to my duties." He stood and stared down at me. "If anything changes, make sure the doctor comes back."

"I know how to look after Holly," Gran said. "Let me show you out, Campbell." She led him to the door, and after a glance back at me, he strode out.

"I got you something." Rupert settled on the seat next to the couch. "I thought you might need distractions while you're recovering." He passed me some recipe books.

"You shouldn't have." I flicked through the top one. "This is great. It's full of medieval recipes."

"They're from our library. I know you like to experiment with old recipes. And I thought these might keep you occupied, too." Rupert lifted the lid on the chocolates to reveal an exquisite range of cocoa dusted truffles.

An intense chocolatey blast hit me. "Thanks, Rupert. You shouldn't have."

"Of course he should. He has manners. He knows how to treat a woman," Gran said. "Lord Rupert, you must stay for dinner."

"Oh, about dinner," I said. "Alice is arranging something. We were going to eat together tonight."

"We'll all eat together," Gran said. "If you'd like to, Lord Rupert?"

"Of course. Dinner would be wonderful," he said.

Alice burst through the front door without knocking. "Holly, where are you? Oh, there you are. Are you still in pain?" She raced over to the couch.

"I'm fine. Everyone can relax. We were just making arrangements for dinner."

"I've done everything. You won't need to lift a finger. Chef Heston is making extra, so we can eat together. I didn't know Rupert would be here, though. He can't have any dinner."

Rupert frowned at her. "I was hardly going to stay away after you told me what happened to Holly."

Alice stuck out her tongue. "I suppose you can stay. Although you can't eat all the roast potatoes. And you can't have seconds for dessert. It's pear crumble, which is one of my favorites."

"Every dessert is your favorite," he said.

"I'll set the table," Gran said. She hurried into the kitchen, the dogs following her.

"Alice, do you realize you're still carrying that skull?" I said.

She patted the skull that sat snugly under her arm. "Of course. I need to get him back to his proper place."

"Which is …"

"In Granny's room. I can't figure out how he got into the old gallery. Granny's particular about who touches him."

Rupert stared at the skull. "I don't know why she keeps that hideous thing around. He should be in the family crypt, along with the rest of our dead relatives."

"You know what Granny's like—she has long conversations with him. She thinks the skull is haunted." Alice shook her head.

"What's this about a haunted skull?" Gran returned from the kitchen.

"My great-uncle Theobald haunts the castle." Alice held up the skull for her to inspect. "He was an absolute rogue when he was alive. The dark sheep of our family."

"That's probably why Granny likes him so much," Rupert said.

Two assistants from the kitchen arrived, and there was a flurry of activity as the food was laid out and everyone sat in their seats.

Rupert helped me into mine, taking care to make sure my ankle wasn't hurting too badly.

"Tell me more about this scandalous great-uncle of yours." Gran served up the beef Wellington and pan-fried vegetables.

"Not many people talk about him." Alice set the skull on her lap and patted it. "He gambled away his fortune and then tried his luck in America. He got caught up in some hush-hush illegal activity. He fled back to England to avoid being arrested."

"None of that's true." Rupert cut into his beef Wellington. "It's all rumors."

"Granny thinks those rumors are true. Anyway, he came back here, claimed to have changed his ways, and joined the priesthood. Two years later, it was discovered he'd gotten three women pregnant. He died of syphilis in a pauper's hospital when he was only thirty."

"That's quite a reputation your great-uncle had," Gran said.

"I find our family history fascinating," Alice said. "I keep telling Holly to get hers done."

"I would, but there's not much to find out," I said. "We don't have any dubious uncles getting women pregnant and running off abroad."

"How do you know, if you don't do the research?" Alice said. "I thought it would be just your sort of thing."

"It's a brilliant idea," Gran said. "While your ankle's healing, you can research the family tree. I've got lots of information about our relatives that could be useful."

"That's genius," Alice said. "It'll stop you from getting bored. I know all the resources to use."

"It's not a bad idea," I said. "Although our family is small. It won't take long to do."

"I'll bring over the things you need first thing in the morning," Alice said.

"Thanks. It could be fun," I said.

"And I've been thinking." Gran raised her fork and prodded it in the air. "You should sue those restorers."

"Why would I do that?" I said.

"Because they caused your accident."

"I'm not suing them. They don't have any money to pay out compensation."

"They absolutely do. Tons of it," Alice said. "Rupert's been involved with this project. Tell them, Rupert. No, let me, you'll only make a mess of things. The restoration is being privately funded. There was some snooty guy poking around before it began, trying to figure out if it was worth investing in."

"He wasn't a snooty guy. That was Solomon King," Rupert said. "He's involved in one of the biggest private equity firms in the country. This work is part of their charitable activities. They like to give back to the community."

"That's even better," Gran said. "Private equity companies are always rolling in cash. Your accident was caused by their negligence. It's only right they pay up. You can barely walk."

"My accident was caused by me not paying attention, Meatball being overexcited because we were about to have dinner, and a piece of pipe. Besides, I'm fascinated by their work. I don't want them to hate me. I was going to ask if I could do some volunteering in my spare time."

"Not with that ankle," Gran said.

"I could sit in a chair and work. I could be useful to them."

"Your gran's right," Alice said. "You need complete rest. You can sit on the couch, research your family tree, and eat those delicious chocolates I've spied. I can't think of anything better. No work for you."

I looked at Rupert for support, but he simply shrugged and shook his head.

I frowned as I stabbed a carrot. I didn't want to be cooped up for days with nothing to do. I loved being out and about.

"You can take that sullen look off your face," Gran said. "Eat your food and think about how to get money out of the investors."

"No, I'm not doing that. But I will rest for a bit." I didn't say for how long, though.

I'd see how my ankle was doing in the morning and then figure out a way to get out of this apartment.

Chapter 3

I rolled over in bed and groaned as I pressed my sore ankle into the mattress.

Meatball jumped up beside me and licked my nose before heading down to my feet and inspecting my injury.

I lay still for a moment, waiting for the throbbing to ease off. I couldn't stay here. I was a terrible patient. If I wasn't busy, I got grumpy. Baking was one of my lifelines. It always kept me occupied and, usually, out of trouble.

"What do you reckon, Meatball? If I call in the reinforcements, I could still get into work. I'll sit in a chair and make lemon drizzle cupcakes all day."

He bounced up to my face and tried to lick my nose once more.

"I agree. It's an excellent idea." I checked the time. It had just gone seven o'clock in the morning. Gran would be fast asleep. She wasn't an early riser, so I'd have the place to myself.

I called Campbell.

"What is it?" he said.

"Good morning to you, too."

"I'm busy."

"Drinking protein shakes and lifting weights?"

There was a silence on the other end of the line.

I suppressed a grin. "I need your help."

"Have you fallen over again?"

"No, and my ankle's much better. And with some assistance, I can get into work."

"No."

I frowned. "Is that a no to helping me?"

"It's a no to all of it. You heard the doctor last night. You need to rest. A sprain doesn't heal in an evening."

"I can rest my ankle when I'm sitting in the kitchen. I'll get bored here on my own."

"You're not on your own. You have your gran staying with you, and I'm sure Princess Alice and Lord Rupert will drop by every five minutes."

"It's not the same. I like to work."

"Holly, there's nothing you can do to convince me to get you out of there. Suck it up and act like the invalid you are. Goodbye."

"Wait!" It was too late. He'd already gone.

I huffed out a breath. "He's so pig headed and stubborn," I said to Meatball. "I expect Campbell's enjoying the fact I can't see what he's getting up to."

Meatball wagged his tail in complete agreement.

I tried Rupert next, but he was most likely still asleep, and didn't answer his phone.

I thought about Alice, but there was no way she'd help me. She got all shrill and red in the face when I tried to convince her I'd be fine to work.

Still, I wasn't giving up. I tested my ankle as I slid out of bed. It was sore, but once I got going, it would ease up.

I navigated to the bathroom, washed, and carefully got dressed so as not to aggravate my ankle. I could do this. This ankle wasn't going to slow me down, and everything else worked just fine.

But I still needed a way to get out of here. Gran wouldn't help me. I could risk the wrath of Chef Heston by calling him and asking for his assistance. He always wanted me at work.

My hand went to the phone, but I paused as I spotted Sara and Justin walking past the apartment.

I pulled up the window. "Hey, over here."

They turned and looked up at me before strolling over.

"How you doing, Holly?" Sara said.

"I'm much better. I want to get into work, but I could do with a hand. My ankle's still sore, and I'm not supposed to put too much weight on it."

"Should you be working at all?" Justin said. "You went down hard on those wet stone slabs."

"I'll be fine. I'm just a bit stiff. Have you got time to help me?"

They glanced at each other.

"We really shouldn't," Justin said. "We don't want to get in trouble. That security guy who carried you out of the old gallery yesterday is terrifying."

"Ignore Campbell. He's all bluster. If you can get me to the kitchen, I'll give you breakfast. Anything you like. On me."

Justin grinned and nudged Sara. "You're on. I'm starving."

I had a feeling the way to Justin's heart was through his stomach.

"Give me two minutes." I limped down the stairs, keeping my weight off my sore ankle as best I could, and scribbled a note to Gran, which I left on the kitchen table to let her know where I was.

I tried to put on my boots, but there was no way I'd get a boot over my swollen foot. I opted for a pair of flat, wide, black shoes. They weren't the fashion choice of the year, but they didn't hurt my foot, and that was all I cared about.

I limped out with Meatball, and we made our way slowly over to Sara and Justin.

"Are you sure you should be doing this?" Sara stared at my ankle. "That doesn't look good. And you're wincing every time you use that foot."

"If I could lean on you both that would be great." My ankle was already shrieking at me to get back to bed.

Meatball raced away, happy to be outside.

"Of course. We all feel terrible about what happened. Loop your arm around my shoulders, and I'll keep you up," Sara said.

"And take my arm," Justin said. "We'll get you there."

"Thanks. I'll be fine in a few minutes." My ankle twinged unhappily as we made our slow way to the castle. I needed a distraction from the pulsing throb radiating up my leg. "How long have you been working for Herbert?"

"Six months," Sara said. "We met through work."

"We were working on a painting from the late sixteen hundreds. It was a family portrait of Eberhard Jabot. It was covered in tinted varnish and had scratches and structural damage all over it," Justin said.

"We had to leave that project because the funding ran out," Sara said. "But I enjoyed it. And if I hadn't been working there, I wouldn't have found Justin."

"Oh! You're dating?" I said.

"That's right," Justin said. "It's nice to be with someone who has the same interests as you."

"It must help," I said. "You can't run out of things to talk about."

"Definitely not. We're both art history geeks," Sara said.

"And your boss doesn't mind you dating and working together?"

"I'm sure Herbert wouldn't mind, but I doubt he's noticed," Sara said. "He always has his head stuck in a book, or is away with the fairies, thinking up some new theory to dazzle people with. He's a great guy, but he gets easily distracted."

"I'd noticed that." I was sweating and seriously rethinking my decision about getting to the castle as my ankle pulsed to the rhythm of my fast heartbeat.

"If you like, we can stop at the old gallery on the way," Sara said. "We spent a few hours there yesterday evening and made great progress. Would you like a look?"

That sounded perfect. It would give me a chance to rest my ankle and get my breath back. "I'd love to see what you've done. And I was thinking I may be able to volunteer if you need any extra hands."

"We always need more people on projects like this," Justin said. "There's never enough money to pay for the staff needed. Historical restoration work is rarely a top priority."

"I found that out the hard way after I came out of university with a history degree," I said. "I couldn't find any work in the areas I was interested in."

"That was a big career change, going from history to baking," Sara said.

"I've always enjoyed baking, and by working here, I can surround myself with history every day. I get to do both of the things I enjoy."

"I'm glad you got into baking," Justin said. "Your cakes are delicious. That lemon drizzle cake is the best I've ever tasted."

"Thanks. It's one of my favorites, too." I limped the last few feet into the east turret, Sara and Justin supporting me.

It was gloomy in the old gallery. The dark red velvet curtains were pulled over the high windows, blocking out the early sunlight.

Sara tried the light switch by the door. "Not again. The fuse must have blown. It keeps doing that."

"It's always the same with these old places," Justin said. "They're not made for electricity. Give me a minute, I'll go and see what's happening. I know where the fuse box is." He hurried away.

I slumped into a chair and stretched out my aching ankle.

Meatball bounded in and raced around before heading to the scaffolding.

"I'll get the curtains open," Sara said. "That'll help us to see. We don't want anyone else taking a tumble." She bustled away and tugged aside the thick curtain that hung over one window.

Meatball barked and whined as he nosed around a bundle of protective coverings left on the floor by the scaffolding.

I blinked as my eyes adjusted to the bright light streaming in through the window. I stared at the large, dark lump on the floor that Meatball was interested in.

Sara headed to the other window and yanked aside the curtain.

My eyes widened and my breath clogged in my throat. I stood on unsteady feet as I stared at the bottom of the scaffolding. "Sara, what's that?"

She turned, her gaze going in the direction I was pointing. Her hand went to her mouth.

Meatball barked, the tone showing his concern as he continued to nose the bundle on the floor.

"It's okay, boy. Come over here." I limp-walked over to him, still not believing what my eyes were showing me.

Sara dashed over and joined me. She sucked in a breath and grabbed my arm. "Is that a body?"

I nodded. It was a woman with dark hair. She was face down on the floor.

"Check if she's okay," I said. From the dark stain on the stones around her head, the injury looked bad.

Sara knelt and pressed a finger to the woman's neck. She recoiled and fell backward. "It's Bluebell Brewster. She's dead."

Chapter 4

The lights overhead flashed on, and I jumped. A few seconds later, Justin hurried in.

"All sorted. It was a blown fuse. I ... What's that?"

"Justin. You'd better call for an ambulance," Sara said.

He jogged over. "That's ... That's Bluebell?"

I inched carefully around the body, making sure not to touch anything. Bluebell's head was twisted unnaturally, her mouth open, and her unseeing eyes fixed on the wall.

"Justin, are you okay?" Sara dashed over to him.

I looked up to see Justin swaying from side to side, his skin ash gray.

"No, I don't think I am." He crashed to the floor.

I pulled out my phone and called Campbell.

"If you think you can get me to come to your apartment, and—"

"It's not that. You need to get to the old gallery. Bluebell Brewster's dead."

There was silence for a heartbeat. "How do you know this?"

"Because I'm here. You'd better hurry."

The line went dead.

"Help is on its way," I said to Sara. "How's Justin doing?"

She tapped his cheek and sighed. "He's dead to the world. He's terrible with anything like this. Not that he's seen a dead body before. But he's a delicate guy. Come on, Justin. You need to wake up." She glanced at the body, her face pale. "What happened to her?"

My gaze went to the high scaffolding. "Did Bluebell ever go up there?"

Sara's gaze followed mine. "Sometimes. She's an expert in historical restoration, although she works more on theoretical ideas than hands-on stuff. It was the main reason we put up with her. She knows what she's talking about. Bluebell was here when we left last night. She said she had work to finish up."

"She was used to working in high places?"

"Yes. But if she'd gone up there, she'd have tethered herself to the scaffolding. We all do. We know the risks if you fall onto something this hard." Sara swallowed and looked away.

I checked over Bluebell's body but saw no sign of a tether around her waist to stop her from falling. I peered at the partially concealed head wound. "I suppose someone could have hit her on the head."

Sara shuddered. "That's horrible. Poor Bluebell."

"Did she have any enemies?"

Pounding feet on the stone floor had me turning. Campbell appeared in the doorway. He strode over. "I thought you said there was one body?"

"Justin's fine. He fainted," I said. "He took one look at Bluebell and passed out."

Campbell was peering at Bluebell's body, when a fast tapping sound reached my ears.

A woman in an immaculate tailored suit that looked designer strode into the room. She wore startlingly high black heels with red soles. Her blonde hair was smooth and her blue eyes sharp.

"What's going on in here?" she asked.

"Oh, Greta." Sara stood and hurried over to her. "We weren't expecting you until this afternoon."

"I had an appointment canceled." She marched past Sara. "What's happening?"

"Who are you?" Campbell turned, blocking her view of Bluebell.

The woman lifted her chin. "Greta Davies. I'm overseeing this restoration project. What business is it of yours? And what have you done to Bluebell and Justin?"

"Greta, something awful has happened," Sara said.

Greta held up a finger to silence her. "Be quiet. I asked you a question." Her gaze was lasered on Campbell.

He puffed out his chest. "I'm Campbell Milligan. I'm in charge of the security of the castle. There's been an incident. You'll need to leave."

"I'm not going anywhere. This is my project."

"This could be a crime scene," Campbell said.

Greta blinked, and her confident manner wobbled before snapping back into place. "What are you talking about?"

"That's what I've been trying to tell you," Sara said. "Bluebell is dead."

Greta's eyebrows shot up. "I spoke to her last night. She was fine."

"We need to get the police involved," I said.

Campbell and Greta both shook their heads, their narrowed gazes locked on each other.

"I'm in charge of this project. I'll deal with this," Greta said.

"You may be in charge of this project, but I oversee security matters," Campbell said.

"Clearly not very well if there's a dead body on the property," Greta said.

Campbell's fingers flexed. "You need to leave. You could be contaminating evidence."

"I'll leave when I choose to," Greta said. "Bluebell was on my team."

I sighed. Now wasn't the time for an alpha stand-off. "Campbell, we really need to let the police know what's happened, even if this was an accident."

"What else would it be?" Greta tried to look around Campbell at Bluebell, but he stepped into her path.

He slid a glance my way. "What are you even doing here? You're supposed to be resting."

"I got bored in the apartment."

"You should have stayed bored. It's safer."

"I wanted to take a look at the work that was done last night." I gestured at the body. "I never expected to find this."

Greta waved a hand in the air and sighed. "Fine. Call the police. I need to speak to my investors about this." She turned and strode away, her phone by her ear.

"I'll make the arrangements with the local police," Campbell said. "Holly, don't touch anything. We need to figure out what went on here."

I lifted a hand. "I won't mess with anything."

Campbell pulled out his phone and walked away as he made the call.

I tried to limp away from the body, but my ankle had other ideas, and I gasped.

"Let me help you. I can see you're in pain. We should never have brought you here. I feel terrible for making you see this." Sara helped me limp back over to Justin.

"Thanks. But it was my decision to sneak out. How are you doing?" I asked. "It must have been a shock to see Bluebell like that."

"You're not kidding. I'm not sure how much I'm processing. I wish Justin would wake up." She shook her head as her gaze went to the door Greta had strode out of. "Trust her to think about the investors' concerns before worrying about Bluebell. Greta has zero interest in history. For her, this is all about turning a profit and showing off to the funders."

I sank onto the floor, glad to get the weight off my ankle. "Wasn't Greta friends with Bluebell?"

Sara joined me on the floor and took hold of one of Justin's hands. "Not that I know of. And Bluebell didn't really do friends. She was ambitious. She put her career before anything else. She had an ambition to become head of the history department at Oxford. Bluebell wanted to get there before she was forty and wasn't letting anything stand in her way. Honestly, it made her a bit of a bitch."

"I noticed yesterday she wasn't friendly with me," I said.

"Don't take it personally. That was just her way. You got used to it after a while. She wasn't into social niceties. If you couldn't help her get where she wanted to go, you were of no interest to her." Sara stroked Justin's forehead. "I learned a lot from her. She was clever. Just not good with people."

I checked Justin's pulse, which was fast, but he was breathing fine. "Was it usual for Bluebell to work alone so late?"

"Yes. She'd often stay late, so I didn't think anything of it last night. Bluebell was always careful, though. She wouldn't have gone up on that scaffolding and messed around. It was always work, work, work."

Greta strode back into the old gallery. "Everything is arranged."

Campbell hurried to join her. "The police are on their way."

She spun to face him. "Is that necessary? This was an accident. Bluebell was always a maverick. She must have made a mistake."

I glanced at Sara. Their versions of how Bluebell behaved didn't tally.

"I'm leading this investigation alongside the police," Campbell said. "We'll determine what happened."

"What a waste of resources," Greta said. "Bluebell must have gotten something wrong. We have high safety standards on our projects. This would have been her fault."

"Your standards can't be that high," Campbell said. "Holly almost broke her ankle in here yesterday."

"And she would be?" Greta said.

I raised a hand. "That would be me."

"Oh, yes. When I spoke with Bluebell last night, she mentioned someone was poking around and getting in the way. You were the one who tripped over our expensive equipment and damaged it?"

"Holly did nothing wrong," Campbell said. "She's been injured. You're responsible."

"I can't be responsible for some clumsy woman who doesn't watch where she's going," Greta said.

"Did I miss my invitation to the party?" Herbert strolled through the door, his white hair fluffy around his face as if he'd forgotten to brush it.

"Oh, no. Don't let him see Bluebell," Sara said in a hushed whisper.

"Greta, you're early," Herbert said.

"It's fortunate I am. You've got a mess on your hands, Herbert." Greta pursed her thin lips. "You know you're on your final warning."

"Err ... I'm not sure what you're talking about. What mess?" Herbert tugged at his shirt collar.

"Bluebell Brewster is dead," Greta said.

Herbert tripped over his feet, his head whipping to the bottom of the scaffolding. He made a garbled sob noise in the back of his throat.

Sara groaned and shook her head. "Greta's as subtle as a sledge hammer. Keep an eye on Justin for me. I need to deal with this." She stood and hurried over to Herbert.

His face was deathly pale. "That's … Bluebell? It can't be."

Sara grabbed his elbow. "Take a deep breath, Herbert. We've had bad news. I came in here with Justin and Holly this morning and we discovered Bluebell dead. It looks like she fell off the scaffold."

He blinked rapidly, then leaned forward and rested his hands on his knees, sucking in great gulps of air. "She's … dead?"

"No one would survive a fall from that height," Greta said. "Bluebell shouldn't have been working in here unsupervised. What were you playing at?"

"Greta, now's not the best time," Sara said.

"I've already warned you to keep quiet. Thanks to your boss's incompetence and Bluebell's clumsiness, this project may close. Then everyone will be out of a job. The funders aren't happy with this news."

Greta didn't seem concerned about the fact someone had died. She was focused on the money and the mess she'd have to sort out. She wasn't going on my nice list anytime soon.

Herbert choked out another sob as he stumbled toward the body. "Bluebell can't be dead. I don't believe it."

Campbell stepped in front of Bluebell's body and shook his head. "I'm sorry, sir. This scene needs to be investigated. You'll be able to see her once she's been taken to the mortuary."

"What investigation? I … I don't understand." Herbert pulled himself upright.

"Ignore Mr. Milligan. He's trying to prove a point," Greta said. "Come with me, Herbert. We have a lot to talk about."

Herbert licked his lips. "I don't want to leave Bluebell."

"You have to. And she won't care if you're here or not. She's dead." Greta grabbed him by the arm and tugged him away. "Sort yourself out. You're supposed to be the project manager, and you're acting like a child." She marched a protesting Herbert out of the old gallery.

Justin groaned, and he opened his eyes. "What happened?"

Sara hurried back to his side and kneeled beside him. "You passed out when you saw Bluebell. How are you?" She helped him to sit up.

He swiped a hand down his face, and his gaze shot to the body. "Oh! It wasn't a bad dream. That really is Bluebell."

"It is. Can you stand?" Sara helped Justin to his feet.

I pulled myself up, trying not to put any weight on my ankle.

"Everyone needs to leave," Campbell said. "This area is out of bounds until I've completed an investigation with the police. And I'll need to speak to everyone here."

"About what?" Justin said.

"Bluebell's death," Campbell said.

"Oh! Um, okay." Justin's eyes widened. "I'll help if I can. Didn't she fall?"

"Let's get out of here. I'll fill you in." Sara caught hold of his arm.

"Don't worry. Campbell just needs to make sure nothing bad happened to Bluebell," I said.

Justin swallowed loudly. "You think this could be murder?" His gaze went to the top of the scaffolding, and he shivered.

"Not for sure. That's why he needs to take a look around," I said.

"There'll be no work for us today," Sara said. "Maybe not any at all if Greta has her way. She didn't look happy."

"Is she always like that?" I walked along beside them slowly as they headed to the door.

"She's usually sharp, but I've never seen her this bad. She worked closely with Bluebell. They didn't like each other much, but there was a professional respect. I can't say for sure, but I got the impression Bluebell reported back to Greta if things went wrong. Greta always knew what we were up to. We could never hide anything from her."

"Which wouldn't have made Bluebell popular," I said.

"Sure, but Bluebell had ambitions bigger than us. She traveled all over the country keeping an eye on sites being worked on. She rubbed a lot of people up the wrong way by telling them what to do," Sara said.

"I don't feel so good," Justin said. "I need to lie down."

"Let's get back to the apartment," Sara said. "I'll make some strong coffee."

"Which apartment are you staying in?" I said.

"We've got the last one on your row," Sara said. "If you need anything, you'll find us there."

We said goodbye, and Sara led Justin away.

I limped back to Campbell. "What do you think?"

"About what?" His gaze was shifting around the scene.

"Do you think Bluebell's death was an accident?"

"I'm keeping an open mind." He turned to me. "Do you think it wasn't an accident?"

"From all accounts, Bluebell was mean. She didn't treat people well."

"I can be mean," Campbell said. "Does that make you want to kill me?"

"Now and again. But it's odd that she was working on the scaffolding with nothing to secure her to it. That would have been dangerous. She's had experience in restoration work. She wouldn't forget to do something like that."

"How do you know she didn't secure herself?"

"There's no tether around her waist."

Campbell studied the body for a few seconds. "If this wasn't an accident, who have you got your eye on?"

"Greta springs to mind. She's not been friendly since she got here. But she wasn't around last night."

"That we know of," Campbell said. "I don't like her."

"Because she's challenging your authority. She's a worse alpha than you."

"There's nothing wrong with knowing you're in charge. It stops people becoming confused. People like guidance and to be told what to do."

"Not everyone does," I muttered. "Just don't let your alpha judgment cloud your head and not look at other suspects. Greta's mean, but there are other choices."

"Like …"

I glanced over my shoulder. "Anyone who worked with Bluebell. Sara was open about the fact that no one liked her."

"You think Sara did it?"

"I didn't say that. But it would be good to talk to her and Justin. And when Herbert's pulled himself together, I should talk to him."

"How about you leave me to interview the suspects in a possible murder investigation?"

I huffed out a breath. "Be gentle with him. He's taken this news badly. And keep me informed. I could be useful."

Campbell opened his mouth as if to object, then nodded. "Agreed. I'll let you know what's going on. You do likewise if you hear anything on the gossip grapevine."

I raised my eyebrows. "People really can change."

He grumbled under his breath. "Don't push your luck, Holmes."

I grinned at him. "I need to get to work. I'll let you know if I hear anything useful." I called Meatball to heel, then slowly limped away from the old gallery and out the main door, using the wall as a crutch as I shuffled to the kitchen.

My head was full of the possibilities of foul play. Had Bluebell Brewster been someone's poison ivy?

Chapter 5

My ankle only throbbed a bit as I sat with it propped on a stool opposite my chair while I peeled a mountain of potatoes. It wasn't my favorite job. I'd much rather be whipping up more lemon drizzle cake, but it was easy, and it meant I got to stay in one place.

Chef Heston strode over. "Is everything okay?"

I nodded. "The potatoes are behaving themselves."

He narrowed his eyes a fraction. "I meant your ankle. Are you in any pain?"

"It's twinging a bit."

"I got you this." Chef Heston produced a frozen gel pack from behind his back. "You wrap it around your ankle and it helps bring down the swelling. I'll put it on for you."

"Thanks. You didn't have to do that." He always managed to amaze me. Most of the time, he delighted in yelling at me and telling me I wasn't working hard enough, but now and again, Chef Heston let a flicker of his caring side peek out.

"I can't have one of my best cake makers incapacitated. We'll get complaints in the café if we run out of your cakes." He strapped the icy blue gel pack around my ankle and then stood.

"Of course. The customers come first."

"I'll bring in the next sack of potatoes." He walked away.

There were more potatoes? I sighed and kept on peeling.

Alice stomped in through the main door. She glared at me as she stopped by the table and jammed her hands on her hips. "You're not my friend anymore."

"Why not? What have I done?"

"You ignored my medical advice to rest your foot, and you didn't tell me about the dead woman in the old gallery." She pulled out a seat and sat on it. "Well, what have you got to say for yourself?"

I repressed a smile. "My foot is being rested. It's healing nicely. And as for the dead body, I'm still figuring that out."

"I had to hear about it from Betsy when she was cleaning out the fireplace. I felt like an idiot. How does she get to know and I don't? This is my home. I must be the first to know about a murder."

"Betsy has a superwoman ability to pick up gossip the second it comes to life. She must have heard about it from the security team. And I was planning on telling you, but I've got my hands full with these potatoes."

"Forget the potatoes. I want to hear about the dead body."

I checked the time. "Give me ten minutes to finish up this lot, then I'll take my lunch break. I'll tell you everything."

"Goody. I'll get us something nice from the café," Alice said. "We can eat outside." She jumped up and flounced away, her blonde curls flying out behind her.

I shook my head as I sped my way through the rest of the potatoes. Alice hated to be left out of anything.

Chef Heston reappeared with a large sack of potatoes in his hands.

"Is it okay if I take my lunch break now?" I said.

He scowled at me. "It's not as if I have a choice in the matter. Princess Alice stopped me and insisted you needed to rest. She chastised me for making you work. I tried to tell her you'd come in without me asking, but she wouldn't hear it."

"I didn't mean to get you in trouble with Princess Alice," I said. "She can be protective."

"Get out of my sight. Go and have your lunch," he said.

I eased my foot carefully off the stool and tested my weight on it. No, it didn't want to work like a proper foot just yet.

I inched my way out of the kitchen and over to the bench where I usually ate my lunch when the weather was nice.

Meatball rolled out of his kennel by the back door and joined me, his tail wagging.

Alice arrived a couple of minutes later and set out a large platter of sandwiches and a tray of cakes, alongside two glasses of lemonade.

"Who else is joining us?" I said.

"Shush. I always comfort eat when I've been betrayed by a friend." She sat in the seat opposite me and grabbed a sandwich. "So, tell me everything."

"There's nothing much to tell. I left my apartment and decided to look in on the old gallery—"

"Hold on. How did you get from your apartment to the old gallery? You were supposed to be resting. I saw you hobbling out here. You can barely walk."

I spent a long time investigating the sandwiches. "I may have had help."

"More secret friends you're not telling me about." Alice shook her head.

"Not secret friends. Sara and Justin were passing. They're working on the project and offered to help me. We went into the old gallery and discovered Bluebell at the bottom of the scaffolding."

"That's what Betsy told me. She said it was a gruesome scene. She's not sure if she'll be able to get the blood out of the flagstones."

"Poor Betsy. I don't envy her that job." I finally took a sandwich and had a bite. "Did Lady Philippa get any hints about this happening?"

Alice sighed dramatically. "No! She's been obsessed with her ghosts lately. And she keeps talking about some bowl going missing."

"A bowl?"

"Yes, she keeps dreaming about it. She's losing her mind. I don't know if she means a cereal bowl or soup bowl. We're getting to the point when we'll have to lock her up permanently and throw away the key before she does damage to the family reputation."

I chuckled, but Alice didn't laugh along with me. I could never tell when she was being serious about locking up Lady Philippa.

"I wish I could get up to visit her, but my foot won't handle all those steps to the top of the east turret. It would be good to pick her brains, see if she had any hint something bad would happen to Bluebell."

"She hasn't mentioned Bluebell to me," Alice said.

"You could go up and have a chat with her. She could have scribbled something down in a notebook and forgotten about it, especially if she's been worrying about her ghosts and this missing bowl."

"I could do that," Alice said. "But on one condition."

"What's that?"

"You take the rest of the day off."

"I don't need to. I'm doing okay."

"No, you're not. You've barely eaten a thing, and you look tired. I'll speak to Chef Heston and get it arranged."

I twisted my ankle carefully and grimaced. Having the rest of the day off wouldn't be a bad thing. I'd been abusing my injured foot, and it wasn't happy.

"Okay. I'd appreciate that. I have overdone it a bit."

"And you had a shock, seeing a dead body. What happened to her, anyway? Was it murder?"

I lifted one shoulder. "Bluebell could have fallen off the scaffolding."

"But you don't think she did?"

"I'm not sure. And Campbell shooed me away from the scene before I could have a proper look. Bluebell could have been pushed, or she fell. Or her death could have nothing to do with the scaffolding, and somebody knocked her over the head with something hard."

"They're all horrible ways to die," Alice said. "I'm sure you and Campbell will get to the bottom of it if anything nasty happened."

"He's being surprisingly open about letting me be involved in the investigation," I said. "He seems more concerned about the arrival of Greta Davies."

"Why? Is she very pretty?"

I grinned. "She's an attractive woman."

Alice crossed her arms over her chest. "Did they flirt with each other?"

"I didn't see any flirting, but he was following her around while she ordered people about."

Color flooded Alice's cheeks. "Does he like her?"

I couldn't tease her any longer. "No. But they both like to be in charge, and he's not happy about that. He could be worried he's about to have his authority challenged."

"Not possible. Campbell is always in charge. He's masterful in every situation." Alice sighed and fluttered her lashes.

I rolled my eyes. "Yes, he's the living dream."

She threw a sandwich crust at me. "Don't be mean, or I won't summon Campbell so he can carry you back to the apartment."

"No way. I'll walk. I can take it slow. I don't want him carrying me around again. It was humiliating the last time."

"He won't mind."

"I will. And he'll definitely mind. Campbell will hold it against me."

"Are you sure you can manage on your own?" Alice ate a sandwich in two bites, then grabbed up the tray. She removed two small sandwiches and a slice of chocolate cake and placed them on a napkin in front of me.

"Where are you going with the food?"

"I have a violin lesson. Mommy heard me perform recently. She said it sounded like a cat had got its paw trapped. Not only do I now have extra piano lessons, I also have extra violin lessons. And I need to hurry, or I'll be late."

"You can't eat cake and play violin."

Alice stood, a glitter of mischief in her blue eyes. "I'm excellent at multi-tasking. Go easy on that foot. I'll catch up with you later. I'll order Chef Heston to give you time off before I go."

"No ordering! Ask nicely."

Alice was gone before I could tell her not to wind up my boss again.

I shared my sandwiches with Meatball and enjoyed the afternoon sun for a few minutes. "Let's test this ankle, shall we?"

He whined and sniffed my leg, a worried look on his furry face.

"I'll be fine. We'll take it slow. And I'll rest if I have to." I sent a quick message to Chef Heston, checking it was okay if I had the rest of the day off.

He sent back a short reply: *Princess Alice insists.*

I felt guilty leaving that sack of potatoes for someone else to deal with, but I was exhausted. I should have listened to everyone's advice and rested for a few days.

I tried a few tentative steps. If I took it slow, and made sure to keep most of my weight on my uninjured ankle, I would make it.

Meatball stayed with me for a short while, giving a whine every time I faltered, but then saw a pheasant dashing across the lawn and raced after it.

I managed about fifty small steps before my ankle gave an unhappy twinge. I took a deep breath and kept on walking.

The twinge turned into a throb, and a sharp pain shot up the back of my calf.

It was time for a sit down. I dropped clumsily onto the grass and stretched out my leg. My ankle was pulsating, and a bead of sweat trickled down the side of my face.

I unwrapped the no longer cold gel pack from my ankle to see if that would help. It didn't.

Meatball raced over and bounced around me, thinking this was a game.

"Go find a stick. I'll throw it for you. I may as well make myself useful until I can walk again."

He raced away, not heading into the trees to find a stick, but back toward the castle.

I flexed my foot and frowned. I could hardly roll home. And I couldn't crawl on my hands and knees. I was stuck.

I pulled out my phone. I wouldn't call Alice for help. She was in the middle of a violin lesson. And if I called Campbell, he'd tell me I was an idiot for walking around.

Meatball's bark had me looking up. He was racing back toward me. Not far behind him was Rupert.

Meatball arrived by my side and wagged his tail.

I petted his head. "You're such a clever boy. I was thinking I needed an extra pair of hands, and you found them for me."

He licked my cheek and then bounded around the grass.

Rupert jogged over. "I knew something was wrong the second Meatball grabbed hold of my jacket and wouldn't let go. He's usually so well behaved."

"Thanks for coming." I held out my phone. "I was just thinking about calling for help."

"Let me get you up. Is your ankle causing problems?" Rupert held out his hands.

"Thanks. It is. I thought it was getting better, but I've overdone it. I was heading back to my apartment to rest." I caught hold of his hand and heaved myself up, balancing on one foot.

"Let me take you back home. Loop your arm around my shoulders, and I'll take your weight." Rupert caught me around the waist and held on tight until I was steady. "Are you ready?" He smiled down at me.

I looked up at him and my heart did a strange little pitter patter. He really was good-looking. He had brilliant sparkling blue eyes and such a warm smile. "Yes. Let's go."

"We'll take it slow. There's no hurry. I was only in the library browsing the collection. I was looking for a new book of poetry. Meatball must have recognized my smell since he came straight in to find me."

"He's been around you a lot. And he likes you," I said.

"He's a great dog. I'd like some of my own, but with the Duchess and her corgi obsession, there's no room. Those corgis rule the roost around here."

"Have you ever thought about getting your own place? You could have all the dogs you liked." I glanced over my shoulder. "Although why would you want to leave when you live in such a beautiful castle?"

"I have thought about a move. The castle is exquisite, but it can get cold in the winter. And I wouldn't mind living somewhere where it was just me and … my dogs. I mean, I don't mind the tourists visiting the castle and looking around, but it doesn't leave much in the way of privacy."

"I didn't think you minded the tourists." We were moving slowly but making progress. I had to admit I didn't mind being held so tightly by Rupert. It gave me a warm glow inside.

"I don't usually, but a few weeks ago, a huge party trampled all over my beautiful herb garden. They took cuttings and left footprints everywhere. It'll take ages to sort out. I wouldn't mind a place that was just my own." He glanced at me, a sheepish look on his face. "I suppose you think that makes me an entitled idiot. I've got all this, but I want something different."

"Of course not. We all have our own version of what would make us happy." I looked up at him and smiled. "You should get your own dogs. The Duchess's corgis will just have to get used to them."

"Nothing can stand up to the Duchess's corgis."

We walked along in silence for a moment.

"Has there been any developments with the death of that young woman?" Rupert said.

"Not that I know of. Campbell's looking into it. Though he's got a challenge on his hands with the project manager. She's as tough as him."

"If I lived away from the castle, I wouldn't be exposed to so many murders," Rupert said. "It's a beautiful place, but it does attract trouble."

"I suppose it does. I've never really thought about that." I had been involved in a lot of crime solving since I'd joined the workforce of Audley Castle.

"Here we are. Your apartment's in sight. How's the ankle doing?"

"It'll be happy when I'm no longer using it. Although having you beside me has made it so much easier."

Rupert blushed. "I'll always help you, Holly. Whenever you need it. Although you're always so together and independent. You never seem to need anything."

"I promise you, I put on a really good front."

We walked for another five minutes, and I was struggling not to gasp for air as I hooked my keys out of my pocket, and we headed along the short path to my apartment.

I unlocked the door, and Rupert helped me inside.

Meatball raced in and went straight to his empty food bowl.

"What's that on the table?" I pointed at the pile of papers that hadn't been there this morning.

"No idea." Rupert helped me over to the table. "Oh! I know what these are. Alice must have been here. It's the information to help you research your family tree."

"I'd better get on with that, or she'll never stop asking if I've done it." I reached for a treat for Meatball.

"Let me." Rupert opened a tin on the side and tossed Meatball a bone shaped biscuit.

"Thanks. He's not really hungry, it's just a bad habit he's got of wanting a treat after a walk." I placed the gel pack on the table and studied the pile of information Alice had left for me.

Rupert peered at a large sheet of paper I'd unrolled. "By the looks of things, Alice has done most of the work for you. She's got your details on here and your gran's. She's traced you back ten generations."

"I had no idea she'd done all this." I eased into a chair.

"She always likes to show off. Can I get you anything for your ankle?" Rupert said.

"Could you put this gel pack in the freezer and get me out a bag of peas? I'll put it on my ankle to help with the swelling."

"Of course." Rupert hurried away and returned with the peas, which he set gently on my ankle. "How's that?"

I winced as the icy coldness bit into my skin. "It'll be good soon. Look at all these names. I didn't know I had so many relatives."

"Hmmm, I recognize that name." Rupert pointed at the name Baron Mistelthorpe.

I looked through the details Alice had written about him. "He was based in Wiltshire. His grandfather was involved in the government, and the title got handed down through the generations. He was a noted soldier, an artist, and a peer of the House of Lords. Alice must have spent ages getting this information."

"It's not his political interests I remember. Unless I've got it wrong, Baron Mistelthorpe had land and money. But he was a scoundrel and had an eye for pretty women."

"How do you know that?"

"I have a great aunt who's fond of researching our family history, too. This baron did business with my family a long time ago. I've seen the old deeds. We bought some of his land when he got in trouble. It was most likely trouble related to the pretty women he was so interested in. I can dig out the information if you like. It could be useful for your research."

"That would be great. I'd like to learn more about my past, even if there is a sniff of a scandal attached to Baron Mistelthorpe."

There was a knock on the door.

"I'll get it," Rupert said. "You stay there." He headed over and opened the door.

Campbell stood outside. "Lord Rupert. I didn't know you were here."

"I've been helping a damsel in distress."

Campbell looked past Rupert and arched an eyebrow. "I'm here because Princess Alice asked me to check in on you and make sure you were behaving yourself."

I smiled and shook my head. "You can tell her I'm fine. But since you're here, is there any news on Bluebell Brewster's death?"

He stepped inside. "Actually, there is. It was murder."

Chapter 6

"Murder!" Rupert stepped back. "What happened to her?"

Campbell glanced at Rupert.

"You may as well tell him," I said. "Campbell, stop looming in the doorway and sit down."

Campbell scowled at me, marched over to the table, and sat in a chair.

"I'll make some tea," Rupert said.

"Thanks. That would be great. So, what happened to Bluebell?" I said to Campbell. "Why do you think it was murder?"

"There are marks on her body that suggest she put up a fight, or at least she was defending herself from an attack. There's bruising on her forearms as if she held them up to ward off her attacker," Campbell said.

"Would you like tea or coffee?" Rupert said. "Holly's got a great selection of herbal teas if you'd prefer one of those."

"Whatever you're making, Lord Rupert," Campbell said.

"Holly, what would you like?"

"I wouldn't mind a chamomile tea," I said.

"Of course. Something to soothe you. I'll get right on that." Rupert hurried over to the kettle and pulled out mugs from the cupboard.

"So, Bluebell had defensive wounds. Was there evidence left behind as to who attacked her?" I said.

"Nothing obvious. And because the scene is a work site, there are fingerprints everywhere. Mainly from Herbert and his crew, but also from the family. There's even some of your fingerprints on site."

"You found that out quickly."

"The local police have been helpful. And I gave them a nudge to speed things up," Campbell said.

"Holly, would you like some cookies?" Rupert said.

"Cookies would be great."

"Um, where do you keep them?"

Campbell gave a quiet sigh.

"The second drawer down on your right," I said. "So what about—"

"Campbell, do you take sugar?" Rupert said.

"No, Lord Rupert."

I bit my lip to stop from smiling and lowered my voice. "Don't get angry with him. He's just being helpful."

Campbell glanced at Rupert and shook his head. "Bluebell was killed between ten and midnight."

"That's helpful. We just need to figure out who went back to the old gallery between those times."

"There are no cameras in that area, so I've got nothing to help there." Campbell's phone vibrated in his pocket. He took it out and sighed.

"Is it something important?" I said.

"Princess Alice keeps contacting me and asking about updates on the murder. I told her there's nothing new, but she's being persistent."

I chuckled. "She did tell me she was good at multi-tasking. She's supposed to be in a violin lesson."

"I know. I hoped it would distract her."

"You should reply to her. I know what Alice is like when she doesn't get a response to her messages."

"Princess Alice doesn't need to be involved with this investigation. And neither does Lord Rupert." His phone vibrated again.

I grinned. "Let me guess, Alice?"

Campbell checked the message, then put his phone on silent.

"She'll hunt you down if you don't answer her," I said.

"Let's focus on the investigation. You were one of the first to find the body. I need your statement. I may as well take it now."

"Sure. Although I'm not certain I've got anything useful to tell you."

"What time did you get to the old gallery this morning?"

"Just before eight."

"And how did you get there? Since you can barely walk, you must have had help."

"As you probably remember, I called you and asked for help, but you rudely said no."

"I rightly said no, given your current condition." Campbell lifted the bag of melting peas off my ankle and frowned. "That has puffed up again."

I tutted at him. "Leave it alone. I spotted Sara and Justin walking past the apartment. I called after them and asked if they could help me."

"How did you convince them to do that?"

"Maybe I didn't have to convince them. They could be nice people who wanted to help someone in need."

"You bribed them. Was it with food?"

I shrugged. "Is that such a bad thing? Justin looks famished every time I see him. I was helping him out."

"Okay, so you got to the old gallery with Sara and Justin."

"And Meatball. He sniffed out the body the second we arrived."

Campbell pressed his lips together. "We know. We've found dog fur on the body. What did you see when you got there?"

"Here's the tea." Rupert placed a tray in the middle of the table and handed out mugs. "So, what have I missed? Oh, I forgot the cookies." He jumped up and hurried away.

Campbell took a sip from his mug and grimaced. "He's given me chamomile tea, too."

"You did say you'd have what he was having," I said. "It's nice once you get used to the flavor."

Campbell took another sip and swiftly put the mug down. "So, what did you see in the old gallery?"

Rupert returned with the cookies and handed them around.

"Thanks, Rupert." I took one and dunked it in my chamomile tea before biting off a chunk. "This is great. I feel much better."

Rupert beamed at me. "My pleasure. It's fun to do the serving once in a while. So, any progress with the murder?"

"That's just what I'm trying to find out, Lord Rupert," Campbell said. He looked at me. "Go on, Holly."

"At first, I saw nothing when we went into the old gallery. The curtains had been pulled over the windows, and when Sara tried to switch on the lights, the fuse was blown. We couldn't see anything. We didn't see Bluebell straight away."

"The wiring in that part of the castle is in bad condition," Rupert said. "That's another reason to move out."

"You're moving away from Audley Castle?" Campbell stared at Rupert.

"Oh! No, well, most likely not. It's just an idea Holly suggested."

"Um, not really. I mean, it was just a thought."

Campbell glared at me.

I shifted in my seat and grabbed another cookie. "I've been wondering about the blown fuse. Is it too much of a coincidence that the lights didn't work, so the body would be harder to find?"

"You think whoever killed Bluebell damaged the fuse box?" Campbell said.

"It's possible. Or they damaged it so Bluebell wouldn't be able to see where she was going. She could have been up on the scaffolding when the lights went out. It would have shocked her. She may even have fallen off."

"The darkness would have given the killer a perfect opportunity to strike," Campbell said. "I'll get the police to check for fingerprints on the fuse box."

"You'll find Justin's on there," I said. "He fixed the lights."

"And plenty of others. There are always contractors coming in and out of the castle," Campbell said. "I doubt it'll get us anywhere, but it's worth a try."

"Have you spoken to anyone Bluebell worked with?" Rupert said.

"Several of them," Campbell said. "Bluebell's respected in her profession, but not many people liked her."

"That's the impression I got of her," I said. "Sara said she was great at her job, but not a people person."

"The killer could be someone she worked with who didn't like her," Rupert said.

"It's possible. And the people she was working with on this project are obvious suspects."

"They're on the list to speak to," Campbell said. "But Bluebell's rudeness isn't a solid motive for murder."

"It would be if she did it often enough and to the wrong person," I said.

"I believe her death is connected to her work," Rupert said.

"What do you mean, Lord Rupert?" Campbell said. "I can't imagine killing someone over a cracked ceiling painting. Surely it's not that important."

"It is!" I said. "It was painted by Witkor Alderman."

Campbell shrugged. He flipped over his phone and pinched the bridge of his nose. "Is there anything else I need to know?"

"Is Alice still hassling you?" I said.

"I've had two missed calls and there are five unread messages from her."

"I did warn you," I said. "You ignore Alice, and she pulls out the big guns and keeps firing until you surrender."

"I should go and see her. She could need reassuring that the castle is safe."

"She'll feel so much better once she knows you're looking out for her."

A muscle in Campbell's jaw twitched, but he didn't respond.

"I don't think there's anything else I need to tell you," I said. "We saw the body, Justin fainted, I called you, and that's it."

Campbell nodded. "Make sure you rest that foot. No work until you're ready."

"Yes, Dad," I said.

He shook his head, grabbed a cookie, nodded a goodbye to Rupert, and left.

"I know murder is gruesome, but this is exciting," Rupert said. "Alice is usually the one who helps you figure out who the killer is."

"It sounds like she's trying to do that, but through Campbell. It's weird that she's stopped getting in touch with me." I checked my phone, but there were no messages from Alice. "I saw her at lunch, and she told me I was a bad friend. Maybe I should have taken more notice. Have I really upset her?"

"I'm sure she'll get around to pestering you once she's got everything useful out of Campbell," Rupert said. "Now, you need to rest. Let me get you into bed."

My eyes widened, and I stared at him. "I, um, I'll be okay on the couch. You can help me over there."

"Oh! Of course. I didn't mean … Well, I would never … I have too much respect for you to suggest anything improper. Not that going to bed with you wouldn't be …" Rupert's words trailed off.

I gave a stilted laugh, my cheeks flaming. "It's fine. The couch is comfy. And I wouldn't mind getting some sleep. I'm sure my ankle will feel better for it."

I removed the bag of defrosting peas from my ankle and gave them to Rupert so he could put them back in the freezer. My ankle looked less swollen but was still sore.

Rupert tucked his arm around my waist and got me over to the couch. He settled me down and helped me get my legs up, putting a cushion under my ankle. "How's that?"

"Perfect."

"I'll bring you the family tree research. If you get bored, you can look at it." He scooped up the papers and brought them over to me, setting them down on the coffee table.

I yawned. "I'll take a look later."

"Is there anything else I can get you? I can always stay. I don't mind."

"No, I'm only going to sleep. I don't want you getting bored. You go back to the library and hunt out your poetry. I've got Meatball to keep me company, and Gran will be home later. She'll look after me."

Meatball hopped on my lap and snuggled next to me, sensing a long nap was on the cards.

"If you're sure." Rupert hesitated, then leaned down and kissed my cheek.

"You've been great. Thanks, Rupert."

"Of course. See you soon. I'll let myself out." He walked to the door, waved at me, and then left.

I touched my cheek where he'd kissed me. Rupert was a lovely guy. A true gentleman.

I sighed. I'd better not get ideas above my station. Even if I had a distant relative who was a baron, it didn't mean I could date a lord.

Meatball snuffled my hand and then laid down, resting his paws on my chest.

I eased down the couch until I was laying with my head on the cushions. "Let's take a nap, Meatball. Maybe I'll get some inspiration about Bluebell's murder while I'm asleep."

Chapter 7

I jerked awake and my eyes flicked open. It was dark. How long had I been asleep?

Meatball was still on my chest. He sniffed my chin, and a low growl rumbled in his chest.

I rested a hand on his back and gently stroked him. "Is everything okay, boy?"

He growled again and then jumped off me and headed to the front door.

I eased myself up and groaned. I'd been laying down for too long without moving.

There was a thick blanket over me. Gran must have covered me up when she found me sleeping on the couch.

I checked the time, and my eyes widened. I'd been asleep for eight hours. No wonder I was stiff.

Meatball continued to growl and sniffed at the front door.

I shifted the blanket and sat up, placing my feet on the floor. I froze when there was a thud from outside.

Meatball's growls grew louder, and he pawed at the door.

The curtain was drawn over the downstairs window, so I couldn't see what was outside making those noises.

I stood carefully and rolled my shoulders to get rid of the kinks from my back. The couch might be comfortable, but it was no place to sleep for long.

I slowly edged toward the door, and my ankle instantly complained.

I'd made it a few steps, when a shadow moved to my right. I grabbed a book from the shelf and held it over my head as my heart thundered in my chest. "Who's there?"

Gran appeared, holding a pineapple over her head. "Holly! You gave me a fright. Why are you sneaking around in the dark?"

I lowered the book. "I'm not sneaking. What are you doing with that pineapple?"

"I grabbed it from the kitchen. I thought it would make a good weapon. I can thrust the spiky leaves in someone's face."

"I heard a noise outside. I was going to take a look."

"Same here. It woke me. Who's out there blundering about?"

"I don't know. Shall we take a peek together?" I gripped the book and edged to the front door.

Gran joined me, holding the pineapple in front of her, the leaves facing out.

There was another thud, and something smashed.

"If someone's breaking your pot plants, they'll have me to answer to," Gran said.

We reached the door, and I eased the lock undone. "Are you ready?"

"Let me at them," Gran said.

Meatball growled again.

I yanked the door open. A looming figure stood outside, dressed head to toe in a long black cloak with the hood concealing their face.

I shrieked and threw the book. It zoomed over their head and landed on the path behind them.

Gran jabbed out the pineapple, trying to hit the intruder with a sharp leaf.

"Wait! Is that Lady Philippa under the cloak?" I stepped forward, squinting in the gloom. The cloak had a velvet lining and bell sleeves. It wasn't the sort of thing your typical lurker in the shadows would wear.

"Oh, no! Have I assaulted a member of the family?" Gran shuffled over and lifted the hood. "It is. Lady Philippa? What are you doing here?"

Lady Philippa didn't respond.

I pushed back the hood. Her eyes were open, but it was like she couldn't see us.

"Is she sleepwalking?" Gran said.

I waved a hand in front of Lady Philippa's face. "She must be. What should we do with her?"

"I heard it's not good to wake someone when they're sleepwalking. It gives them a shock, waking up suddenly and not knowing where they are or how they got there."

"And Lady Philippa has a weak heart. We don't want to scare her to death." I touched her arm, but she didn't respond. "Let's get her inside. We don't want her wandering away from the castle and getting lost."

We stood either side of Lady Philippa and guided her into the apartment. She came willingly enough, if a little slowly.

I shut the door behind us. Gran led Lady Philippa into the living room, where she settled her in a chair.

We stood side-by-side and looked down at her. Meatball and Saffron snuffled around Lady Philippa's feet, curious about this new, unresponsive arrival.

"What do we do now?" I said.

"Offer her a coffee?" Gran said. "Maybe you should call Alice or Rupert. They may know what to do with her. Does she often do this?"

"No. I didn't even know she sleepwalked."

Lady Philippa groaned and jerked upright in the seat. "Oh! What's going on? Where am I?"

I knelt beside her. "Lady Philippa, it's Holly. You're in my apartment."

She blinked several times. "Holly? How did I get in here?"

"We think you've been sleepwalking, Lady Philippa," Gran said.

"Ah! Yes, that would make sense. I do have bouts of sleepwalking when I'm under stress. I've had terrible business to deal with lately."

"You gave us a scare," I said. "We thought someone was trying to break into the apartment."

She looked around. "You have a lovely home. You should invite me over more often. Since I'm here, may I have a cup of tea?"

"Of course," Gran said. "I'll go get that for you." She glanced at me before hurrying into the kitchen.

"What's making you so stressed?" I asked.

"You! I've been worried about you. I haven't seen you for months. And I heard about your injury."

"Lady Philippa, I visited you four days ago. And I can't get up the stairs at the moment because of my sprained ankle."

"Really? Such a short time. It seems like much longer. My family is so neglectful of me, I'm left alone for days."

I knew that wasn't true. "I'll get up to see you again soon."

"You're such a good girl. How is your injured ankle?"

"It's not great. I overdid things today. But don't worry about me. I'll be fine now I'm following the doctor's advice and resting."

She patted my hand. "I'm glad to hear it. But it's not just that keeping me up at night." Lady Philippa tugged the cloak around her shoulders. Underneath it, she wore dark red velvet pajamas.

"What else is worrying you?"

"I had a disturbing dream."

I settled on the couch. "What was the dream about?"

She smoothed a hand over her hair. "It was confusing. My ghosts have been demanding my attention, bothering me whether I'm awake or asleep."

"What are they worried about?"

"The work in the old gallery. I didn't want it to happen, but I was overruled by the rest of the family. The ghosts hate the disturbance. They love routine and order. They like peace. It's why they spend so much time with me. But ever since that noisy crew started work on the painting renovation, we've not had a moment's peace."

"I'm sorry to hear that. The work is fascinating, though. You should take a look. You should tell your ghosts there's nothing to worry about."

"They have a right to worry. The work is disruptive and not useful."

Gran returned with a mug of tea for Lady Philippa and settled next to me on the couch.

"Thank you." Lady Philippa took a sip.

"So, your dream?" I said.

"Yes, my dream. That young woman was definitely killed in the old gallery. I saw her get pushed." Lady Philippa gave a nod.

"Goodness. You were there when it happened?" Gran said. "Have you told the police? Did you see who pushed her?"

"No, but someone chased the victim up the scaffolding," Lady Philippa said.

"How would you know that if you weren't in the room?" Gran said.

"I dreamed it three nights ago."

I squeezed Gran's elbow, giving her a gentle warning not to push too hard. She was always the pragmatist. She'd have little time for ghost stories. "Lady Philippa has this ... ability. She can sense when bad things are about to happen."

"Of course she can't. That sounds made up," Gran said.

"It's true. I've predicted a number of bad things that have happened in Audley Castle. I only missed Bluebell's murder because I've been so distracted with my own problems."

"You can't dream about something that hasn't happened," Gran said. "Or if you could, you'd be in some circus, showing off your talents to the world."

"My social standing doesn't allow me to perform in a circus," Lady Philippa said. "Although it sounds fun. I'd love a go on a trapeze."

Gran sniffed. "If you say so, but it seems suspicious to me. You probably heard people talking about it."

"No. I dreamed it." Lady Philippa glared at her. "Are you doubting my word?"

"Gran, I could do with some hot chocolate. Would you mind making me some?" I said.

Gran glanced at me and sighed. "I can take a hint. Fine, I'll go make hot chocolate." She headed into the kitchen again.

"Sorry about my Gran," I said. "She only believes in things she can actually see. She's got a practical head on her shoulders."

Lady Philippa waved away the comment. "I have no problem with your gran. She's a fun lady. And I've spent my life having people ridicule my ability. But I know the truth, and that's the main thing. And I know Bluebell Brewster was killed."

"You're right. Campbell has found evidence to suggest that. There was a struggle before she died."

"Yes! Whoever wanted her dead was chasing her. She was terrified. I felt her fear."

"Did you hear any noises or fighting that night? Your bedroom is over the old gallery."

"No, the walls in the east turret are so thick, you can't hear anything in the next room, or below you. It's one of the reasons I chose that place as my permanent home."

"Did your dream give any clues as to who attacked Bluebell?"

"No, but they chased her up the scaffolding. And they were fast. Bluebell must have thought she'd been cornered, or figured they wouldn't follow her. But they climbed up after her and shoved her off." Lady Philippa sighed. "What a terrible way to die. My ghosts are so unhappy. The murder has unsettled them. What with the restoration work and now this death, I'm not sure I'll be able to make them happy ever again. And I don't want them to leave. I'll be all alone in my turret if they abandon me."

"You won't be alone for long. Once my ankle is better, I'll start visiting you again."

She patted my hand again. "Of course you will. I can always depend on you for treats and good company."

Lady Philippa turned the mug in her hand and then placed it down. "I've been worried about something to do with this murder. I wasn't sure if I should say something to Campbell about it."

"What's been worrying you?"

Her gaze dipped. "I care very much for my ghosts. I don't want them to get in trouble."

"I can't imagine why they would. What is it?"

She sighed. "Since they've been disturbed by the restoration work, some of them have been angry. I was thinking, is it possible that one of my ghosts chased Bluebell and killed her?"

My eyebrows shot up, and I stared at Lady Philippa. The expression on her face suggested she was serious. "Um, I know you believe in ghosts, but they aren't real. They can't hurt people."

The lights blinked out, and I gasped. There was a thud, and something hit my foot.

I held in a squeak of alarm.

"Sorry!" Gran called from the kitchen. "That was my fault. I used the dodgy plug socket. Give me a minute, I'll get it sorted."

I sat in the dark, not moving. Something had touched me when the lights went off. I edged out my foot and felt something hard. I decided not to move until the lights came back on.

Gran's footsteps approached, and she headed to the fuse box. A minute later, the lights flared on.

"All sorted," Gran said as she returned to the living room. "The hot chocolate will be ready in a minute." She headed back into the kitchen.

I looked on the floor. There was a book by my foot. I picked it up and inspected the title. *A Haunting Guide to the Ghosts of Audley Castle* by Amelia White.

I held it up. "How did that get there?"

Lady Philippa looked at the book title and smiled. "Are you sure there's no such thing as ghosts?"

I turned the book over. "I don't get it. Did you put it there? Did it fall from a shelf?"

She shook her head and picked up the mug. "I'll make you a believer one day. But first, you have a murder to solve."

Chapter 8

"That should keep these two tired for the rest of the day." Gran walked through the front door with Meatball and Saffron on their leashes.

I looked up from the breakfast table where I was sitting eating a bowl of muesli. "Thanks for walking Meatball."

"Of course. I'm happy to help. And you need to rest your ankle. How did you sleep after our late-night visitor?" Gran hung up her jacket and unclipped the dogs' leashes.

"Not great. Lady Philippa gave me a proper scare. I kept thinking about everything she told me."

Gran put two bowls of dog food down on the floor and then joined me at the kitchen table. "Me, too. And all that strange talk about ghosts and premonitions. She's not serious, is she?"

I glanced over at the book of ghost stories that had appeared last night. "I have to admit, I'm not so sure anymore. Everything got a bit spooky."

"A blown fuse and a book getting knocked off the table is hardly spooky," Gran said. "Don't let her strange ways bother you. You're much too sensible for that." She stood and switched on the kettle. "What are you going to do today?"

"Don't be angry, but I'm going to work. My ankle feels better. I'll take it easy and only do light duties."

"Don't let Chef Heston work you too hard," Gran said. "And don't go poking around any sites where you'll hurt yourself again."

I finished my breakfast. "I'll take it easy, I promise."

I left the apartment and made my way slowly into work, settled Meatball in his kennel, and then hobbled into the kitchen.

Chef Heston glanced up as I entered. "I should put you on peeling duty again, since you only did a half day yesterday."

I wrinkled my nose. "Whatever you think best, chef."

He grunted. "We're out of lemon drizzle cake. Get to work on that, or I'll get complaints from the customers."

I grinned as I pulled on my apron, sending a silent thanks to everyone who loved my lemon drizzle cake so much.

A few hours later, Louise walked past with a trolley laden with food.

"Hey, Louise. Where are you going with that?" I rolled my shoulder, my arm stiff from all the whisking.

"Chef Heston told me to take this to the restorers." She frowned. "I hate going into the east turret. It's always spooky and cold. It gives me the shivers."

I wiped my hands on a clean cloth. "Let me take it. I don't mind going in there."

"Are you sure you're up to it? What with your dodgy ankle."

"I'll take it slow, and I can lean on the trolley. I want to see if they've started work again after what happened to Bluebell. It's been a big shock for them all."

Louise shuddered. "That's another reason to stay away. A woman died in there. I've never understood your obsession with crime."

"Um, it's not an obsession."

"Really? How many murders have you gotten tangled up in since you've been here?"

I shrugged. "One or two."

"One or two dozen, more like."

"I'm not that morbid. I just have an interest in justice. And I'm also interested in seeing how the painting restoration is going."

"If you say so. But it doesn't appeal to me. Neither does that creepy old place. Give me a bright, freshly painted new build any day. If you want to do it, the job's all yours."

"Great. I'll take it over in a few minutes. It'll save you from getting creeped out."

Louise shrugged and walked away.

I finished what I was doing, then took the trolley and wheeled it slowly out of the kitchen and over to the east turret. By the time I got there, my ankle wasn't happy, but it was holding up.

I wheeled the trolley as far as it would go, then picked up two trays of sandwiches and took them up the steps into the old gallery.

Sara and Justin stood together, mixing up something in buckets. Herbert was scratching his head and looking at paperwork, while Greta stood to one side, her phone by her ear as she tapped her foot and scowled.

"Lunch is here," I said.

Justin turned and grinned. "Great. I'm starving." He hurried over with Sara, and they took the sandwiches from me.

"There's cake on the trolley," I said.

"I'll go get that." Justin loped away and returned with the cakes.

"How's your ankle doing?" Sara said around a mouthful of sandwich.

"It's getting better. I wanted to see—"

"Don't stand around gossiping." Greta marched over. "You're paid to work, not eat."

"We're entitled to a lunch break," Sara said.

"Did somebody say lunch?" Herbert walked over. His eyes looked red, as if he'd been crying, and his hair was even messier than usual.

"You'd better grab a sandwich before Justin eats them all," Sara said.

"Ten minutes, and then you're all back to work." Greta strutted away and pulled out her phone again.

"She doesn't seem too happy," I whispered to the others.

"The funders have been on her back about what happened to Bluebell," Sara said quietly. "Greta's been snapping and snarling at everyone all morning."

"She must be stressed," I said.

"We all are. But we're not being mean to everyone else," Sara said.

"I've been keeping out of her way," Justin said. "She's almost as sharp as Bluebell." His gaze went to the spot Bluebell's body had been discovered, and he shuddered.

"Maybe Greta's hungry. I can get snappy when I haven't eaten. I'll take her a plate of food," I said.

"Don't say we didn't warn you. She's being horrible to everyone," Sara said.

I selected two sandwiches and a large slice of lemon drizzle cake and walked over to Greta.

Her head snapped up as I approached. "Can I do something for you?"

"I thought you'd like some lunch. Everyone needs to take a break."

She glanced at the food, then finished typing out a message on her phone. "That cake looks all right. It's not stale, is it?"

"I baked it fresh this morning. It's lemon drizzle. A specialty of mine."

Her lips pursed as she dragged her attention from her phone. "You made it?"

"I make most of the desserts for the castle."

"I suppose if the Audley family like your food, it can't be that bad."

"I've never had any complaints." I passed her the plate.

Greta hesitated, then took it. She glanced back at the others. "If they worked as fast as they ate, we'd be much farther along."

"When can you get back to work on the painting restoration?"

Greta ate a bite of lemon drizzle cake and nodded. "It should be tomorrow. We can only do prep work today. I don't know why there's such a holdup. We could start today, but that overly officious muscle head who acts like he owns the castle has claimed we can't interfere with the crime scene. You see, he's put up barriers to stop anyone getting near the scaffolding."

"If you mean Campbell, he's always thorough with his investigations."

"He's interfering with my project. And despite what he keeps telling me … hold on a minute." She lifted her phone and sighed before whizzing off another message. "Where was I? Oh, yes. I can't believe it was murder."

"Bluebell wasn't having problems with anyone before she died?"

Greta slid me a glare. "Not problems. But she seemed worried about something."

"What was she worried about?"

Greta scrolled through her phone for several seconds. "She didn't give me the details, and I wasn't interested enough to ask."

"Could someone she worked with have been causing her trouble?"

She glanced back at the group and sneered. "Bluebell had a thing for older men. Especially the men who could get her places. Although there's only about ten years between her and Herbert."

I stepped back on my injured foot and winced. "Bluebell and Herbert were in a relationship?"

Greta lifted a finger as her phone rang. "Bear with me. Hans, if I have to tell you which shipment to send out one more time, you're fired. Yes! The blue folder. Send three copies. Do it now." She ended the call. "I'm going to be twice as busy thanks to Bluebell dying. It'll take months before I can get a replacement."

I stuffed down my sarcasm as best I could. "That must be stressful for you. You were saying about Bluebell and Herbert?"

"Don't sound so surprised. It's still a man's world, despite what all the equality nonsense tells you. Bluebell had ambitions. I know where she wanted to work. It wasn't for me, overseeing the projects I secured funding for. This job was simply a stepping stone to higher ambitions."

"That didn't bother you?"

"Why should it? As long as she did what I asked her to. I've done it myself plenty of times when I needed to move up the career ladder. You grit your teeth and do what you have to, in order to get where you need to be."

"Bluebell had a relationship with Herbert because she thought it would gain her a promotion?"

Greta looked up from her phone screen. "I never said that. But despite Herbert looking like an idiot, he's a genius. He's been working in this field for decades. If he doesn't know something about restoration, it's not worth knowing. That makes him an effective ally. And people like him. I find him intensely irritating, and his inability to complete reports is driving me crazy. But Bluebell must have seen something in him worth pursuing."

"Could he have gotten her the job she wanted at Oxford?"

Greta's eyes narrowed. "What do you know about that?"

"Oh! I don't know anything. Not really. It's just that the others said she wanted to work there."

She lifted a shoulder. "Herbert does have connections at that university. I imagine Bluebell was using their relationship to get to them."

I looked back at Herbert. He'd just dropped half a sandwich down his shirt and was scraping it off with a pencil. I couldn't imagine a less likely couple. Would Bluebell have used Herbert to get a boost up the career ladder?

"I hope your project's not held up for too long, what with everything that's going on," I said.

"This is a minor hiccup. It'll get sorted, and everyone will be happy."

"It's being funded by a private equity firm?"

Greta placed down her slice of lemon drizzle cake. "You do like to find out everything that's going on. You're a proper little snoop."

"I couldn't help but take an interest. I love history. I was excited when I heard what was planned for the old gallery. It'll bring the place back to life."

"Most likely. But how did you find out about our investors?"

"Rupert told me."

"Lord Rupert Audley told you this information?" She huffed out her disbelief.

"That's right. I'm friends with the family."

Greta snorted a laugh, then her expression grew shrewd. "Really? The Audley family know who you are?"

"Yes. They're kind to all their employees. I know them well. I spoke to Rupert and—"

"You speak directly to Lord Rupert?"

"I do. He's a nice man. In fact, he helped me when I injured my ankle after falling over in here."

Her gaze flicked to my foot. "Oh, yes. We're not accepting responsibility for that if you're angling for some kind of payout."

"No, I'm not. I don't want anything like that. I just want to see this restoration completed."

Greta sniffed. "It will be. Viking Investments plan to invest in many community projects like this. It's an excellent way to raise their community profile. They're a company that likes to give back. So many of these companies amass wealth and hoard it. Viking is different. If this goes well, we'll hold corporate events here, maybe even make use of the castle as a function venue for wealthier clients. I'm sure this place will appeal to those who have investments with the firm."

"You don't think Bluebell's death will cause a problem? Not everyone thinks murder is a good thing."

"If it even was murder." Greta shook her head. "You know what they say, though. All news is good news." Her phone rang, and she answered the call, walking away and abandoning her plate of food.

I watched Greta strut around in her high heels as she talked on her phone. There was a motive there. If this murder was leaked to the national press, it could get a lot of coverage for Audley Castle and, potentially, Viking Investments. Would it be the kind of coverage her firm would want? How far would Greta go to get publicity for them?

I'd have to keep an eye out to see if any members of the press showed up. If they did, Greta was going to the top of my list of suspects.

I bit my bottom lip. I hadn't asked her for her alibi. I'd have to leave that to Campbell. He'd be thrilled to go toe-to-toe with Greta again. It sounded like they'd had a few run-ins that I'd missed.

I raised a hand as I headed to the door.

Sara and Justin waved back.

"Thanks for the food," Sara said.

"Any time." I hurried away as best I could with the trolley. I needed to get back to work before Chef Heston missed me.

My next target in this investigation had to be Herbert. He didn't seem to be handling Bluebell's death well. He'd burst into tears when he'd seen her body, and now there was the possibility he'd been sleeping with Bluebell.

Was Herbert simply a guy in touch with his feelings, or had he been having a relationship with Bluebell? And if he had, had that relationship soured, and he'd done something unforgivable?

Chapter 9

I gave a big yawn as I pulled off my apron, hung it up, and then headed out of the kitchen. "Come on, Meatball. Let's take one last look at the work in the old gallery. Gran will have to walk you tonight. My ankle's not up to it."

He bounced out of his kennel by the back door and raced away.

I limped after him, stifling another yawn. Who'd have thought that hurting your ankle would make you so tired? I was ready for a hot bath and another early night.

My ankle gave a sharp twinge, and I leaned against the wall, taking a moment to catch my breath.

"Are you still pretending your ankle isn't a problem?" Campbell appeared in front of me. He leaned against the wall and crossed his arms over his chest.

"I never said it wasn't hurting. But I've never had a sprain this bad before."

"You should be resting."

"And you should be investigating Bluebell's murder."

"Why do you think I'm here?"

I looked up at him. "Have you found out anything useful?"

"I always find out useful things."

I shook my head. "I talked to Greta Davies today."

"What a treat."

"She's not much fun to be around. But I got something interesting out of her."

"If you're going to tell me Bluebell and Herbert were dating, I've already heard that rumor."

"Do you believe it? It's a bit odd. They make a strange couple."

"I've seen odder couples work."

"I suppose so. What do you think about Greta?"

He grunted. "I never swear in front of a woman. But Greta tries my patience. Let's leave it at that."

"She's sharp, that's for sure. When I was talking to her, she kept being interrupted by phone calls and messages. I got the impression the company supporting this restoration is pushing for results."

"Viking Investments. I know about them, too."

"You have been busy. When were you going to tell me all of this? You did say you'd keep me informed."

"I'm informing you now. And I'm a busy man. I don't just have this investigation to deal with. The Duke is planning a weekend away, and the Duchess wants to fly to Aspen next week for charity work."

"It's a tough life being so in demand."

"I haven't even mentioned what Princess Alice wants to do."

I grinned. "Greta said something that got me worried. She suggested that Bluebell's murder could be good for business."

"How would that work? People won't come here while there's a killer on the loose."

"Greta thinks it'll be good publicity. Maybe she wants the press to snoop around and ask about Bluebell's murder. While they're here, she could promote the restoration work and the funding from Viking."

"It's a cold move, but it would work," Campbell said. "Flip the bad news into something positive. I can imagine her exploiting that."

"Have any members of the press been in touch to ask about what happened to Bluebell?"

"No one's been in contact. I would know," Campbell said.

"We should keep an eye on that. If any members of the press start sniffing around, then Greta could be involved in this."

Campbell rubbed his hands together, a gleam in his eyes. "I'm warming up to making her the prime suspect. And she doesn't have a great alibi."

"That's something I forgot to ask. Where was Greta when Bluebell was killed?"

"In bed, asleep. She lives alone. No surprise there."

"Don't be mean. Maybe Greta is too busy with her career to have the time to put up with a messy, clumsy man in her life."

"Yeah, that would be it," Campbell said. "Anyway, she claims to have been asleep. I'll keep looking into her movements, see if she's been lying to me."

"What about Herbert?"

"I'm also interested in him."

"He could have found out that Bluebell was using him and they fought. Although he seems like a nice guy. I imagine he'd be heartbroken rather than angry if he found out she'd been using him."

"That's why I'm here. I was just going in to see Herbert to discover how nervous he gets when questioned," Campbell said.

"I'll come with you."

"No. You can barely walk. You should go home."

"I'm fine."

"No, you're not."

"I know my limits. I've been doing much better today."

"Which is why you were gasping for breath and hanging off the wall to stop from falling when I found you?"

"I wasn't that bad."

"Walk up those steps without wincing." He pointed to the three stone steps leading into the east turret.

"I can do that. No problem."

"Go on then."

I scowled at him. He was like the annoying big brother I'd never had.

"And you can't limp while you do it."

"I'll limp if I want to."

Meatball raced out of the old gallery. He cocked his head at me and wagged his tail before bounding away.

"Meatball doesn't think you can do it," Campbell said.

"Not true. Meatball thinks I'm capable of anything." I shuffled over with as much dignity as I could muster. I made it up one step, almost without limping. I turned back to Campbell. I hated to admit defeat. "You can always give me a piggyback."

"Not a chance. My back's still aching from the last time I was forced to carry you."

"You're such a charmer." I stopped on the first step.

"I'm waiting."

"You're putting me off because you're watching."

He sighed and strode to my side. "Take my arm. I'll help you up."

"I'm not an invalid."

"Actually, you are. Stop being so stubborn."

"I'll stop being so stubborn when you stop being so childish."

"Just do it, Holly. We have a murder suspect to grill."

There was a yell from inside the old gallery just as I'd made it up the second step. "That sounded like Herbert."

Campbell dropped his hold on my arm. He jumped up the rest of the steps and raced into the old gallery.

"Don't mind me. Leave the invalid behind. I'll just hobble along on my own."

The shouting grew louder as I limp-walked into the old gallery.

Herbert stood in front of Sara and Justin, his face red. "I told you not to touch those things. They're nothing to do with you."

"I'm sorry, Herbert," Sara said. "I didn't want them getting any of the paint restorer on them."

"They're not yours to touch." Herbert was clutching a small pouch against his chest.

"What's the problem?" Campbell strode over to them.

"They touched her things." Herbert's finger trembled as he pointed at Sara and Justin.

"What things?" I joined Campbell. "Has something been stolen?"

"No!" Justin shook his head. "Sara didn't mean any harm. We needed extra space, and Bluebell's tools are still lying around."

"I simply gathered them up and put them in her work pouch," Sara said.

"Bluebell paid a lot of money for these tools," Herbert said. "They were important to her."

"I didn't think you'd mind," Sara said. "I should have asked if it was okay to move them."

"I do mind. I'm in charge. I tell you what to do. You shouldn't have touched them. Bluebell wouldn't like it." Herbert's jaw wobbled, and tears filled his eyes.

"Perhaps you two should call it a day," I said to Sara and Justin.

"Yes, good idea," Sara said, casting a concerned look at Herbert. "We were just doing some prep for tomorrow. I'm really sorry, Herbert."

He waved her away. "Just go."

Sara grabbed Justin's hand, and they hurried out of the old gallery.

Herbert heaved out a sigh. "They don't understand. They're too young. They think everything is so easy."

I glanced at Campbell. He was glaring at Herbert like he'd just caught him committing a horrifying crime.

"Sara and Justin seemed sorry. From what I know of them, they're good people. They wouldn't do anything to damage Bluebell's tools." I stepped forward and touched Herbert's elbow. He was shaking.

He let out another big sigh, and his shoulders sagged forward. "I know. I'm tired. I haven't been sleeping much since Bluebell died. I still can't believe it's true."

"I'm guessing Bluebell didn't like anyone else using her tools?" I said.

Herbert lowered his hands to show the pouch he held. "She was so proud of these. She had her initials engraved on the handles."

"I'm sure you'll look after them for her," I said.

Campbell cleared his throat and gave me a pointed stare.

I ignored him. Herbert was distressed. He needed comfort, not bullying by Campbell.

"I will. I'll look after them. She loved her work. It ... It was all she loved."

"Would you like to talk about Bluebell?" I said.

Herbert shook his head. "I can't."

"You have to," Campbell said.

He straightened his shoulders. "It's a bad time. Greta keeps yelling at me about some report I'm supposed to finish, but I can't get my thoughts together. Every time I focus on the paperwork, I keep seeing Bluebell lying over there."

"You shouldn't be working. Her death has badly affected you," I said. "Can you take time off?"

"No. Greta wouldn't like it. And everyone else is getting on with things. I don't want to let the side down."

"I still need to speak with you about Bluebell. You need to make time for that," Campbell said.

Herbert's shaking intensified. "I don't feel well. There's so much to do. I keep thinking about Bluebell and what she'd like for her funeral. Her family is non-existent. I don't want anything to happen to her that she wouldn't be happy about."

Campbell sucked in a breath as if to continue his blunt attempt at questioning. The guy had zero compassion.

"How about you get something to calm Herbert's nerves?" I said to Campbell.

He stared at me. "Like what?"

"Would you like something to drink?" I asked Herbert. "Shock affects people in different ways. You need to be kind to yourself at a difficult time like this."

"I'm not sure. I can't remember the last time I had a break."

"Sit down." I gently guided Herbert to a nearby seat.

He let me lead him without any protest. "I do need to rest. And a strong coffee would be nice."

"You sit here for a minute." I walked away, caught hold of Campbell's elbow, and led him out of Herbert's earshot. "Be gentle with him. You can see he's upset."

Campbell's eyes narrowed. "I can also see he's a suspect in a murder investigation."

"Which doesn't mean you get to railroad him. Go get some coffee and sugar cookies from the kitchen. When he relaxes, he'll be more open to your questions."

"Why don't you get the coffee?"

"Because I'm trying to calm down the suspect, not get him so riled up he runs off, or collapses."

"Fine. Just don't cause trouble while I'm away." Campbell marched out of the old gallery.

I headed back to Herbert, who was slumped in the chair. "I'm sorry about Bluebell. Were you close?"

He scratched his fingers through his hair. "Not really. She was clever and worked hard. I only ever want the best work from my team. Bluebell knew what she was doing, but ..."

"But what?"

He glanced away. "She could be difficult. She was always suggesting new ways of doing things."

"Is that a bad thing?"

"It usually was. I've been in this business a long time. I'm the first to admit I can get set in my ways, but Bluebell was always challenging me, undermining me, and making me think my work wasn't good enough."

"You didn't like her because of that?"

Herbert fidgeted with the tool pouch. "I liked her results. She created immaculate restorations. But Bluebell could be abrupt. Some people called her rude behind her back."

"Did you think she was rude?"

He was quiet for a few seconds. "Bluebell could be superior. She acted as if she knew everything. She had the best education, so I can't blame her for that. And she probably was the smartest person in the room when we were all together, but you don't always want your nose rubbed in that. I told her once or twice to be kinder to the others, but she laughed in my face. She said if they couldn't keep up with her that was their problem. Bluebell wasn't dumbing down for anybody."

"Herbert, I hope you don't think this next question is intrusive, but I've heard people say you were in a relationship with Bluebell."

He stared at me. "Dating? Oh, no. I mean, she was an attractive woman, and clever. But we weren't even friends. We worked together."

"You didn't go on a single date?"

He chuckled and looked around the room. "I have one true love in my life. That's my work. It keeps me busy. I've never really considered marrying. My poor wife would have to put up with being second place to my love of art history and restoration. There aren't many women who'd do that. And neither should they."

That was odd. Was Herbert lying? Or had Greta been stirring things up to draw attention away from herself by alluding to Herbert's fake relationship with Bluebell?

"Have you been asked about where you were when Bluebell died?" I said.

"Not yet. I expect that's what your security man wants to talk to me about." He sighed. "I didn't mean to fall apart. I wasn't expecting the questions. And I was angry with Sara and Justin. That was my mistake. I was wrong to yell at them. I'd been meaning to clear up Bluebell's tools, but …" He lapsed into silence and stared at the tool pouch.

"Once you've done that, it makes everything so final. It means she's really gone."

"Exactly. Bluebell won't walk in tomorrow with a determined gleam in her eye and tell me I'm doing everything wrong. I almost miss her scolding me." He stroked a hand over the tool pouch and then set it to one side. "It's silly."

"No, it's not silly. Even if you weren't that friendly with her, you respected what she did."

"Of course. I always admire someone who can restore damaged art work, even if I don't particularly like them."

"What time did you stay working in the old gallery the night of Bluebell's death?"

"I was here until almost nine that evening. Greta left first. She had a business meeting in London, I believe. Then Justin started talking about how hungry he was. Sara was complaining because they had to finish their work and then go and get food because he hadn't gone shopping.

They left before me. I stayed to finish up what I was doing."

"And where was Bluebell?"

"She was up on the scaffolding when I left."

"Did you see if she was tethered to the scaffolding?"

"Of course. We all know when we go up there to use the safety measures. I must admit, I occasionally forget if I'm excited about something. Bluebell was always the first to march over and demand I attach my tether. She was never lax when it came to things like that."

"After you left here, what did you do?"

"I've got the apartment two doors along from Sara and Justin. I went back there, did research online, and went to bed. I took my laptop with me. I wanted to research lightweight vacuum cleaners, so we had one on the scaffolding to clear up any mess. I fell asleep, and that was it."

"Did anyone look in on you when you were in your apartment?"

He shook his head. "I know, it's not the greatest alibi. But I'd never do anything to hurt Bluebell. Even though she interfered with my working methods, I was glad she was around. It's good to have someone to nudge you and make you think about different things. I miss her terribly."

Meatball bounded over. He had something pink hanging out the side of his mouth.

"What have you got there?" I went to take it out of his mouth.

"Oh! That's one of my cleaning rags. You can't have that." Herbert lurched forward and yanked the pink cloth out of Meatball's mouth.

Meatball barked a couple of times, not happy to have his discovery taken from him.

Herbert stuffed the cloth into his jacket pocket. "He shouldn't go around chewing on rags. We use all kinds of chemicals in here. It's not safe for him."

"Sorry. He was only showing off his find." I petted Meatball to keep him quiet.

He still wanted the rag. He gave one more disgruntled bark, then raced away.

Herbert smoothed his hands over his hair. "I just don't like to think of him getting sick, that's all. We've had enough tragedy around here."

Campbell walked through the main doorway and over to us. "The coffee is on its way."

Herbert jumped from his seat. "I don't have time for any more questions. I've told your assistant all I know. And I'm really not feeling too good. I have a headache."

"But I have questions for you," Campbell said, shooting a glare my way. "My *assistant* may have forgotten to ask you something important."

Herbert pointed at me. "Holly can tell you everything I know. I must go." He hurried away, grabbed his backpack, and raced out the door.

Campbell stared after him. "Has he forgotten there's a murder investigation going on?"

"Sit down. Herbert was talking to me before you came back. I'll tell you everything."

"Then all my problems are solved." Campbell took the empty seat Herbert had vacated. "So, what did you find out?"

"Herbert's devastated about what happened to Bluebell. He didn't stop shaking the whole time I was talking to him."

"Shaking because he is sad, or shaking because he's scared he's about to get charged with murder?"

"He's shattered. It's genuine. But the most interesting thing I discovered was that he wasn't having a relationship with Bluebell."

"He told you that?"

"He did. I asked him about it. Herbert said they hadn't even been on a date. He's basically married to his job."

"Herbert shared the same passion as Bluebell. Wouldn't that be a match made in heaven?"

"He said otherwise."

"Did you believe him, or is he covering his tracks?"

"I'm not sure. You think he'd have been proud to date Bluebell. She was young, smart, and attractive."

"And Herbert's not exactly the catch of the decade. He had a food stain on his shirt."

I thumped his arm. "To some women, he's the living dream. But if they were having a relationship, he's a great liar. And he wasn't faking how shaken up he was about her murder. I think he really misses her."

"Which suggests he had feelings for her that weren't returned," Campbell said.

"It's possible."

"And his alibi?"

"It's as bad as Greta's. He's staying in an apartment near mine. He left here just before nine that evening, went back to the apartment, did some work online, and fell asleep. No one saw him."

"That's not a decent alibi," Campbell said. "We could take his laptop and check his internet history. That could help to rule him out."

"It's worth a shot. But he's definitely sadder about Bluebell dying than Greta is. All she cares about is how this will affect the project's success and if her boss is happy."

"They both stay on the suspect list," Campbell said.

Meatball bounded over again. He had another object in his mouth. This time, it was a bright red cloth.

I reached down and eased it out of his mouth. "Herbert told you not to keep stealing his cleaning rags. They could make you ill."

Campbell grabbed the cloth from my hand and held it up. "This isn't a cleaning rag. It's a pair of women's panties. Are these yours?"

Chapter 10

I choked out a laugh as I stared at the frilly red panties in Campbell's hand. "Of course they aren't mine. Why would I leave my underwear lying around in here?"

Meatball bounced up and down, trying to get the panties back from Campbell.

Campbell glanced at the ceiling. "You don't think they're Lady Philippa's? Could Meatball have snuck up the stairs and grabbed these from her drawers?"

"Don't even joke about that. And he wouldn't go up there on his own. He's not a fan of that staircase, and Horatio is mean to him if he goes in without me."

Campbell held the underwear up to the window. "Chantelle's Secrets. That's an expensive brand. This is real silk and lace."

"You know a lot about women's underwear."

He slid a glance my way. "Sure."

"Do you buy a lot of ladies' underwear?"

He shrugged. "Only for the right woman. Who do these belong to? It must be someone with money to burn."

I peered at the panties. "No offense to Sara, but they look a bit small for her."

"They'd fit Greta," Campbell said. "She's skinny enough to get into these."

"Or Bluebell," I said.

"What have you got there?" Rupert ambled into the old gallery, his hands stuffed in his pockets.

Campbell hid the panties behind his back. "Lord Rupert. I didn't expect to see you here."

Rupert's forehead wrinkled. "I was taking a stroll and wanted to see if the restoration had started up again. What are you both so interested in?"

"You may as well show him," I said.

Campbell frowned and revealed the underwear. "We were trying to figure out where these came from."

Rupert glanced at me. "They're very pretty. Are they yours, Holly?"

"No! Why do people keep asking me that? I don't leave my knickers lying around for Meatball to grab hold of."

Rupert's cheeks flushed. "Of course not. I was just thinking how nice they were. They'd suit you."

I closed my eyes for a few seconds and rubbed my forehead. "I promise you, they're not mine. Meatball found them." I looked at Meatball. He was staring intently at the panties in the hope that Campbell might throw them for him.

"So ... why the interest in them?" Rupert said.

I looked around the room. "Meatball turned up a few minutes ago with a pink cloth in his mouth when I was talking to Herbert. Herbert grabbed it and stuffed it in his pocket before I could see what it was. I thought I saw a flash of lace but figured I was mistaken. You don't use lacy things as cleaning rags."

"Meatball found more than one pair of women's underwear in here?" Campbell said.

"He could have done. And it was underwear Herbert didn't want me to see," I said. "Campbell, show Meatball the underwear again. Let him have a sniff."

"Why would I do that?"

"Because he could lead us to more. Or at least reveal where he found them."

Campbell lowered the underwear to Meatball's nose so he could have a good sniff.

Meatball grabbed them and raced to the other side of the room. He dropped the underwear on the floor and looked back at us.

We all followed him.

"This was where Herbert's backpack was. He grabbed it before he left." I stared at the space on the stone floor. "Did the underwear come from his bag?"

Rupert cleared his throat. "I'd like to suggest a theory. It's not so uncommon for men to like women's underwear."

"I'm not sure that's true, Lord Rupert," Campbell said.

"You don't like admiring an attractive woman in her undies?" I grinned at Campbell.

Campbell scowled at me.

"Um, I didn't mean that. I have an old school friend who … well, he wears women's underwear. He says it keeps everything snug and in the right place," Rupert said.

My eyebrows shot up, and I glanced at Campbell. "Have you got any experience of this?"

"Of course not. But I suspect Herbert has this underwear for another reason."

"What would that be?" I said.

"A fetish?" Rupert said. "I have another friend who likes to drink champagne out of a woman's shoe after she's worn it all day."

I stared up at him. "You have strange friends."

"That's a public school education for you. It gives you a chance to experiment."

"I was thinking more like a trophy," Campbell said. "We need to know more about Herbert. I'll run a full background check on him. Maybe this unusual behavior has gotten him in trouble in the past."

"A knicker stealer. There are worse crimes. Although the women missing their knickers won't be happy. Especially if they're expensive," I said.

"If they're Bluebell's panties, it could give him a stronger link to her murder," Campbell said.

"Herbert killed Bluebell for her knickers?" Rupert said. "He must have a serious fetish."

"I don't think he murdered her for her frillies," I said. "I'd like to talk to Sara, though. Maybe she's had underwear go missing. Or if Herbert was being a problem for Bluebell, she may have confided in Sara."

"From what we know about her, I doubt Bluebell confided in anyone," Campbell said.

"It's still worth an ask. I'll go catch her now before it gets too late." I limped toward the door.

Rupert was instantly by my side. "You need to rest your ankle. I see you're in pain."

"It's not so bad." I gritted my teeth, hoping he wouldn't hear my lie.

"Campbell, help me make Holly see sense," Rupert said.

Campbell sighed. "That's enough for tonight. You'll mess up your ankle if you keep using it."

"And you need to take it easy," Rupert said. "The ladies' knickers will wait until the morning."

"But we need to find out what's going on now. Why is Herbert hoarding ladies' underwear? What if they're Bluebell's?"

"We'll find that out tomorrow," Campbell said. "I'll run the background checks this evening, and we'll know more first thing in the morning."

"You do need to relax," Rupert said. "Rest your foot. You don't want a relapse."

"I can't relax. There's a killer on the loose."

"Take this." Campbell pulled a ball out of his pocket and handed it to me.

It was bright red and had a woman's face on it. I gave it a squeeze.

"It's a stress ball. I find it useful," he said.

"This can't work. You're always stressed," I said.

Campbell shook his head. "It'll keep you occupied, especially since you can't work out with that bad ankle. Now, time for you to get home."

Rupert pulled his puppy dog eyes on me. "Please, Holly. I'll worry all night if you don't rest."

I lifted my hands. "Okay. I give in. I'll rest."

"See you in the morning, Holmes," Campbell said.

I reluctantly limped away with Rupert supporting me. I may be resting my ankle, but my brain definitely wouldn't quieten down. Not until I figured out this underwear mystery and if it was connected to Bluebell's murder.

❧❧❧❧❧ ☙☙☙☙☙

"Men are such strange creatures." Gran sat opposite me while we ate breakfast the next morning. "It doesn't surprise me one bit to hear Herbert's been hoarding women's panties."

"We don't know for sure that's what he's been doing. But it is odd. We need to find the owner of the panties. They could be connected to Bluebell's murder."

"Some men keep trophies of their conquests. Perhaps that's what Herbert's been doing."

I wrinkled my nose. "Campbell suggested that. But Herbert's no Lothario. He's a nice guy, a bit eccentric and obsessed with history, but there's nothing wrong with that. He's not a cad."

"Intelligence is an attractive quality to many women. Maybe he lures his conquests in with exciting talk about historical scandals. He gets them in bed and takes their underwear as a prize. As I said, men are strange."

"Ray's not strange."

"Ray's lovely, but he's definitely odd. He spends all his time in that smelly potting shed, he talks to his plants, and he keeps bringing me herbs." Gran gestured to the full windowsill where half a dozen assorted potted herbs sat. "I keep telling him I have a black finger when it comes to gardening, but he's convinced he'll find something I can keep alive."

"That's sweet. He's a good guy."

"I know it. I'm a lucky lady." She collected our empty bowls and placed them in the sink. "He's even dropped a few hints about us getting a place together."

"I wondered why your search for an apartment had stopped. Are you considering it?"

"Maybe. I don't know. Call me old-fashioned, but I like to be married before I do anything as serious as getting a place with a man."

"It's not old-fashioned. It's great. But it'll be awhile before he proposes, won't it?"

"I imagine so." Gran turned back to the sink. "Anyway, I need to get these dogs out for a walk. I'll drop Meatball off at his kennel outside the kitchen when I'm done."

"Great. Thanks for doing that. I should be okay in a couple of days to walk him again." I pulled out the stress ball Campbell had given me and gave it a squeeze before placing it on the table.

"What have you got there?" Gran walked back to the table.

"Campbell gave it to me. It's one of those squeezy balls that's supposed to be good for relieving stress."

She lifted it up and turned it around. "Why does it have your face on it?"

I took the ball back and stared at the woman's face. It did look worryingly like me. "That's not me."

"Yes it is. You pull that puzzled expression when you're thinking hard about something." Gran chuckled. "Did Campbell have it made especially with your face on?"

I glowered at the ball. Campbell was a dead man if this really was a picture of me. "I'd better get to work." I stood and shrugged on my jacket.

"Take it slow. No running any half-marathons today." Gran followed me to the door.

"Nope, I'll stick to slow limping and cake baking."

We said goodbye, and I slow walked toward the kitchen.

I sent a message to Alice while I was walking to see if she wanted to grab lunch later. I hadn't seen her for a couple of days, which was unusual.

The response came back immediately. *No. Busy.*

I put away my phone. Whenever there was something going on in the castle, Alice was always poking around, trying to find out what was happening. And she insisted on knowing everything about any mystery. Maybe she was busy enjoying her new violin lessons.

I had no time to think about Bluebell's murder, missing underwear, or stress balls with my face on, as I headed into a bustling kitchen.

I got to work, and the next few hours passed in a flurry of whipping up batches of cake for the castle visitors who'd be coming through all day.

I'd just placed a batch of lemon drizzle cake in the oven, when Meatball started barking.

I glanced around to see if Chef Heston had heard. He was fine with Meatball being around, so long as he didn't cause a distraction.

Meatball continued to bark. He sounded more excited than annoyed.

I hurried outside to quieten him down.

He was bouncing up and down, wagging his tail as Sara petted him.

"Hey! I didn't mean to overexcite your dog. I just wanted to say hello to him. He's a cute little guy," she said.

"He's great. He's my best friend."

"I can see why," Sara said. "He's so cute, aren't you, puppy?"

Meatball rolled over and exposed his belly for a stroke.

Sara laughed and happily obliged.

"I'm glad I've seen you," I said. "I wanted to ask you about Bluebell and Herbert's relationship."

Sara looked up at me. "Their relationship?"

"Yes. How serious was it between them?"

She bit her lip and focused on Meatball, scratching behind his ears. "I don't think they had a relationship. Not really."

"I was told they were together."

"Who told you that?" Her smile faded. "Let me guess. Greta. She loves to stir things up."

"It may have been her. It isn't true?"

Sara tilted her head from side to side. "I don't know much about it. Bluebell was a private person. But I overheard her on the phone a few weeks ago. It sounded like she was talking to someone about a new job. She said she wasn't happy with her current boss."

"Bluebell was leaving the company?"

"Possibly. She never said anything to me, but I could tell she wasn't happy about something. She was being meaner than usual."

"She never said anything about Herbert hassling her?"

"No, nothing like that." Sara stood and brushed her hands together. "I think Herbert would have liked a relationship with Bluebell, but they weren't together. I got the impression he creeped her out. He didn't do anything nasty, but he was always getting her coffee and trying to chat. You met Bluebell before she died. She was never one for small talk. If anything, Herbert had a crush on her, but he didn't get the hint she wasn't interested."

"It makes sense now why he was so upset when he saw her body," I said.

"I feel sorry for him. I like Herbert, but he has zero clue when it comes to women. He was driving Bluebell away by being clingy, and he didn't even realize it. I said something to him about Bluebell only being interested in her work in the hope he'd get the message. It didn't change the way he acted around her."

"Would Bluebell have used Herbert's interest in her to further her career?"

Sara's mouth opened and then snapped shut. Her forehead wrinkled. "It's possible. I don't know, though. Bluebell was clever enough to get where she wanted to go without using people. I mean, not in the sense that she'd sleep with a guy to get what she needed. I hope not, anyway. Do you think that's what she was doing?"

"No, I've no proof of that. But Herbert's connected. Maybe Bluebell decided to take advantage of that. Especially if he was hassling her. She figured she could get something out of the situation."

Sara blew out a breath. "I suppose so. And Herbert was being persistent on the night Bluebell died. We were packing up to leave, and only Bluebell was still working. I suggested to Herbert that he come back to the apartment with me and Justin to have something to eat, but he kept finding excuses to stay. It was obvious he wanted to talk to Bluebell when there was no one else around."

"Would you say he was hassling her that night?"

"I wouldn't call it hassling, but he seemed determined. He kept looking over at Bluebell and getting this wistful look in his eyes. I should have told him he was wasting his time, but there'd have been no point."

All this information was confirming my suspicions about Herbert. He could have grown desperate because he was obsessed with Bluebell and she rejected him.

"This will sound odd, but has any of your underwear gone missing while you've been working on this project?" I asked.

Sara laughed. "You're kidding?"

"Meatball found some underwear in the old gallery. Two different pairs of knickers. I'm looking for the owner."

"I'm sure I haven't lost any pairs of pants. What do they look like?"

"Pink and red, made of silk and lace."

Sara patted her rounded stomach. "I'm not missing anything that looks like that. I'm a big knickers kind of girl. The lacy stuff doesn't hold everything in. When you do a physical job like this, you need everything to stay where it should."

I smiled at her. "I thought I'd ask. They looked expensive."

"Then you can definitely count me out. I buy my undies from the bargain bin. And I'm glad Justin's not interested in seeing me in frilly underwear. He'd only be disappointed by my giant pants." She petted Meatball on the head again. "I'd better go. We're working on cleaning a large section of the ceiling painting today, and I need to make the most of the light."

"I hope it goes well," I said. "I'm looking forward to seeing the finished result."

"Me too. See you later." Sara walked off toward the old gallery.

The more I learned about Herbert, the more worried I became. He was a lonely guy, obsessed with a beautiful, ambitious woman who wouldn't have given him a second look.

Had his desire for Bluebell driven him over the edge? She'd rejected him one too many times, and he'd snapped?

Add in his odd collection of women's underwear, underwear that could have belonged to Bluebell, and things weren't looking good for Herbert.

Chapter 11

I slowly limped home after my day working in the kitchen. I called Alice to see what she was doing, but her phone went to voicemail.

I sent her a message. *How's everything going? What are you up to? It would be nice to see you.*

I'd sent three messages during the day. She hadn't replied to any of them. It was unlike her. She was always great at keeping in touch.

Meatball barked and raced ahead of me. He was chasing someone who was jogging around the lawn in front of the castle.

As I got closer, I saw it was Campbell.

Meatball was running after him, barking to get his attention. Campbell was ignoring him.

But Meatball was persistent. He kept on running, wagging his tail, and giving the occasional excited bark. Only the coldest of hearts could have ignored that for long.

His determination paid off. Just as Campbell completed a circuit of the lawn, he grabbed a stick and hurled it for Meatball.

Meatball gave a happy bark and raced away to collect it.

Campbell jogged over to me. He was barely breathing heavily and hadn't even broken a sweat. The man was a machine.

"Are you jealous?" Campbell said.

"Of what?"

"The fact that I can run, and you can barely walk."

"You can be a big jerk at times. Has anyone ever told you that?"

"Only you."

"Maybe only me to your face," I said.

"No one else would ever dare." He grabbed the stick Meatball had returned to him and threw it again.

"What have you learned about Herbert?" I said.

Campbell's phone buzzed in the arm strap on his bicep. He checked who had sent him a message, then started stretching. "It's just as I thought. He's straight-laced. He's got two PhDs and is highly respected in his profession."

"What about his personal life?"

"He doesn't have one. He never married and has no children."

"Any criminal record for stealing women's underwear?"

"If he's been doing it, he's never gotten caught with the panties stuffed in his pocket," Campbell said. "He's never even had a parking ticket."

"Do you think that's too good to be true?"

"He's a nervy kind of guy, but a killer? I'm not so sure." His phone buzzed again.

"Do you need to check that?" I pointed at the phone strapped to his bicep.

"Nope. I know who it is."

I shrugged. "I get the same impression about Herbert as you. But everything I'm learning about him from other people is making me wonder. Could he simply be a lonely guy who's terrible at reading signals from women, or is he hiding something darker? Love does crazy things to people. Herbert could have gotten spun around when Bluebell started working with him. He fell for her but got repeatedly rejected. It must have been hard to accept."

Campbell grunted as he stretched out his quads. His phone was now buzzing every few seconds. "He's got no alibi for the time of her murder."

"He has an alibi, but it's not one we can check out," I said.

"Unless I can get hold of his laptop," Campbell said. "And without evidence to implicate him, I won't be able to see the information I need."

"You could ask Saracen to work his magic."

"You're suggesting I get a member of my team to hack into his laptop?"

"It won't be the first time you've done it."

"Allegedly."

"It's an idea. If we can't find anything to pin on him, we may have to do that."

"If he did it, he'll crack. Herbert's under pressure. It must feel like we're closing in on him every hour."

"Maybe that's why he's so tense."

"The confession will come if he's guilty, especially if he killed the woman he loved, and I've eliminated all other suspects. It'll leave him in the spotlight."

"Have they been eliminated?"

"Not yet."

I stared at his buzzing phone. Someone really wanted Campbell's attention, and he didn't want to give it to them. "What's troubling me is that I'm hearing conflicting stories. Some people say Herbert and Bluebell were an item. Sara says they weren't, but I reckon Herbert had a huge crush on Bluebell."

"If he's been taking her underwear, that suggests an interest from him, even if Bluebell didn't feel the same," Campbell said.

"Or he has a weird fetish he needs to deal with," I said. "Sara told me something worrying, though. The night of the murder, Herbert stayed behind so it was just him and Bluebell working in the old gallery."

Campbell's phone rang. He pulled it out of the strap, gave a sigh, and then answered it. "Princess Alice."

I grinned. It made sense now why he was ignoring the messages. Alice was after him for something.

His mouth twisted to the side as he listened to her.

"Let me talk to her when you're done," I said. "I've been trying to reach her all day."

Campbell turned away. "Yes, Holly's here. We're talking about the investigation."

"Can she see us? Where's Alice?" I peered at the castle. We weren't so far away that she couldn't see us from inside.

"We're still looking into the suspects," he said. "You don't have anything to worry about. You're safe."

"Campbell, let me talk to her," I said. "I think my phone is broken. She's not replied to any of my messages. Ask her if everything is okay."

He continued to ignore me. "I understand. Of course. You'll know if there's any danger."

I reached for the phone, but he jogged away from me.

"Hey! That's not fair. I can't chase after you with this ankle. Let me talk to Alice."

With a final nod, Campbell turned back to me and held out his phone.

I took it from him. "Alice, what have you been doing all day? I've been sending you messages. I … Hello? Are you still there?" I looked at the display on Campbell's phone. The call had been disconnected. "Did you do that?"

He shook his head as he took back his phone. "She said she couldn't talk to you right now. Princess Alice is busy."

"Doing what?"

"Studying."

"Studying for what?"

"I couldn't tell you. She's been in the library since dawn. She didn't even have breakfast."

"But she never misses breakfast. She loves breakfast food. Well, any food, but especially waffles. Does this have to do with her music exams?"

"You have to stop asking me about Princess Alice. I don't question my employer's behavior. Neither should you."

"You should question her. Alice is being weird. And she never misses a meal. Is she sick?"

"No. And she's no weirder than usual."

"I'll tell her you said that."

He was silent for several seconds. "Holly, maybe it's time you took a step back from the family."

"Why? Has Alice said something to you about me?"

"No, this isn't about Princess Alice."

"Then why would I want to take a step back?"

"You're very close to them."

"And …"

"And you work for them."

"I know that. I don't expect anything from them. I like being friends with Alice and Rupert."

"Yes, I've noticed how friendly you've been with Lord Rupert."

"You sound jealous."

"I sound concerned. You'd make an odd couple if you ever got together."

"Don't be rude. It wouldn't be weird if we dated. Not that I'm saying that would ever happen." My cheeks felt warm, and I looked away.

"It would be weird. You work in his kitchens."

"He doesn't care about that. And weird couples work. I wouldn't automatically put Justin and Sara together, but they seem happy."

"They work together. Justin isn't Sara's boss."

"Technically, the Duke and Duchess employ me, so Rupert isn't my boss." I frowned at him. "And you can't lecture me about my relationships. What about you and Alice?"

His gaze narrowed. "What about us?"

"Does she call any of the other security and question them the way she does you?"

"Sometimes. And I am hired to protect her. She has a right to question me."

"Does she gaze at them like she does you?"

A muscle in his jaw flexed. "I've not noticed. And even if she did, it would be irrelevant. There are some lines you don't cross."

"I still don't know why you're bothered. Maybe I have a tiny crush on Rupert, but it's not serious. I've done nothing wrong. Neither has he. We're friends. Nothing more."

"All I'm saying is don't get all gooey-eyed over Lord Rupert. As we're witnessing in this investigation, getting involved with someone you work for is a bad idea. Herbert fell for Bluebell, and she rejected him. They were still forced to work together every day. If that was what tipped Herbert over the edge—"

"I have no plans to kill Rupert simply because dating him would be complicated." I pursed my lips. "But I do see how Herbert's situation would have been tricky."

"And it'll be hard on you, if you let anything happen between you and Lord Rupert."

"What aren't you telling me? Why do you care about my relationship with Rupert all of a sudden?"

He cracked his neck from side to side. "Because we have a friendship, of sorts. It mainly involves you irritating me and me trying to stop you from doing anything reckless, but it works."

"We're really friends?" I grinned at him.

"Not always. Just be careful."

"Why? Have you heard something? You wouldn't be warning me off unless there's a good reason."

"I've given up on warning you off of doing anything you shouldn't a long time ago. You never listen to me."

"I do sometimes. I'm listening to you about this. What is it?"

Campbell glanced around. "You may as well know. The Duke and Duchess received a communication from Lord Rupert's parents. They're lining up potential matches for him."

"Matches! They want to arrange his marriage?" My heart plummeted. "That still happens?"

"They think he needs a nudge in the right direction. His parents don't want him to get too comfortable as a bachelor. They've got several eligible women lined up for him to meet."

I gulped. "Has he got any clue this is about to happen? Shouldn't we warn him?"

"That he's about to go on dates with lots of attractive, well-groomed, high-class women? It's hardly going to be a chore for him."

I huffed out a breath, jealousy fizzling inside me. "It's not as if he needs to form an alliance to strengthen the family. They're already ridiculously wealthy and influential."

"We move in different social circles to them. He was raised to do this. Marriages are still made that are advantageous to influential families."

"What's wrong with being a bachelor, anyway? I enjoy being a bachelorette."

"You're a spinster."

"You say that like it's a dirty word. There's nothing wrong with being a modern, independent woman."

"I'm sure there isn't. I'm not debating that with you. But Lord Rupert's about to have a lot thrown at him. If you get in the way and influence his decisions, you won't be popular. You may even find yourself looking for a new job if his parents discover what you've been up to."

I lifted my chin. "I haven't been up to anything. Rupert is free to choose who he likes."

"No, he's not. If it were that simple, I'd be with …"

My eyes widened, and I sucked in a breath. "Go on, say it. You'd be with Alice. You do like her. Have you ever said anything to her?"

Campbell pressed his lips together and narrowed his eyes.

"Campbell, it's just the two of us and Meatball out here. I'll admit that I'm fond of Rupert, if you do the same about Alice."

He crossed his arms over his chest and looked away. "We have good lives here. We don't want to do anything to muddy the waters. You stick to the kitchen, and I'll stick with the security detail."

"What if our hearts don't want to do that?"

"Then *your* heart will get shriveled up and miserable. And if Lord Rupert's parents find out a kitchen assistant is messing with their son's future happiness, they'll cut it out with a silver spoon."

"They wouldn't? With a spoon?"

He grunted. "Most likely."

"They want him to be happy, though," I said.

"Can you make Lord Rupert happy?"

I grabbed the stick Meatball had returned and hurled it as far as I could. It had been a long-held fantasy of mine that one day I'd date Rupert. But that fantasy was in my head. I'd never acted on it. I never thought I would. Was I about to lose Rupert to some refined, stunning, upper-class beauty? My heart didn't like that idea one bit.

"How about we stick to murder for now?" I said. "This relationship business is messy."

"As I suspect the relationship between Bluebell and Herbert was just as messy. Mixing work and love is complicated," Campbell said.

"How far would someone go to fix the problem of unrequited love?" I said.

"On a personal level, let's hope neither of us ever have to find that out," Campbell said. "I'll keep digging into Herbert's background. He doesn't have much of a social media profile, but there could be something there that triggers a warning. And I have loose ends to tie up with the other suspects, such as they are."

"I'm going to find Alice," I said. I needed some girl time. I had to share what I'd found out about Rupert. Maybe that was why she was keeping away from me. She was terrible at keeping secrets and didn't want to tell me the bad news that he'd soon be off the market.

Campbell shrugged. "It's your funeral. She was highly strung this morning. She doesn't want to be disturbed."

"Alice won't mind me dropping in. I often use the library. I can see what she's doing."

"Don't say I didn't warn you," Campbell said. "About a lot of things."

I hobbled away with Meatball, my head a mess of complicated relationships and tricky love situations.

For now, I couldn't fix the issue of Rupert's upcoming romantic liaisons, but I could focus on what had happened between Herbert and Bluebell.

The trouble was, my heart had other ideas. All I could think about was Rupert and his marriage to a society beauty. I liked myself well enough, but I wouldn't stand a chance against someone like that.

Did I even want a chance with Rupert? I should stick to the fantasy. I couldn't risk everything I had. I loved my life working in the kitchen and living in my little apartment with Meatball and Gran, even though it got a bit crowded at times. If I took a risk on Rupert, I'd lose everything. I'd have no home, no job, and probably no reference. And if Rupert's parents came after me, silver spoon or not, I wouldn't last five minutes.

"Let's stick with what we know, Meatball," I said. "There's no point in causing problems. We've got a good life. We aren't lonely, are we?"

He looked up at me and lifted a paw, giving a little whine. It seemed he didn't agree with me. Or maybe he was just hungry.

I limped into the castle and headed to the large family library. The Duke and Duchess had been gracious in giving me access to their exquisite collection of books. I made regular use of their generosity and would often borrow books to read in the evening.

I tapped on the door and poked my head around the side.

Alice was sitting at a desk, leaning over a book and scribbling on a notepad beside her.

"Hey, what are you up to?" I said.

Her head shot up, and she squeaked. She shoved back her chair and raced to the door. "You can't be here."

I staggered back at the sharpness in her tone. "I didn't mean to interrupt. Is everything okay?"

Alice shoved me back until I was outside the library. "I keep telling you, I'm busy. Stop bothering me." She slammed the door in my face.

I stared at the closed door. Had I just been unfriended?

With a heavy sense of dejection pressing on my shoulders, I limped home.

Chapter 12

"Holly! Focus on your work. Those lemon drizzle cakes won't put themselves in the oven." Chef Heston stomped past, a scowl on his face.

I glanced down at my neglected bowl of cake batter. "Sorry, chef."

"What's the matter with you? You've been wandering around with your head in the clouds ever since you got here this morning."

I focused on the cake batter before giving it a hearty whisk. "Nothing. Everything is good." It wasn't. I couldn't stop thinking about what happened with Alice yesterday, or the news about Rupert's love life.

I'd sent Alice a message last night to say sorry for disturbing her, but she hadn't responded. That only made me feel worse.

Chef Heston shook his head. "How's that ankle doing? Is it still causing you pain?"

"Oh, no. It's not that that's bothering me. My ankle is much better," I said.

"Good. Then go to the storeroom and get these supplies." He handed me a long list of baking goodies.

I did need a break. My head wasn't in the baking game, and I didn't want to make a mistake with the ingredients. I poured the cake mix into half a dozen loaf tins, then placed them in the oven.

I headed outside and over to the supply storeroom next to the kitchen. I unlocked it and headed inside. I was heaving out a large sack of flour when I spotted Justin heading toward the old gallery.

I raised a hand and waved at him.

He smiled and ambled over. "I hope you have some of your delicious cakes left over today. I keep dreaming about your lemon drizzle cake."

"I've just put a batch in the oven. I'll set some aside for you," I said. "How's everything going with the restoration?"

He adjusted a bundle of books he carried under one arm. "It's going well. I can't stop, though. I need to finish taking pictures of what we've been doing. Herbert needs them for a report."

"It sounds like you're making progress."

"We're getting there."

I gritted my teeth as I tried to lift the flour, and a groan slid out as I put too much weight on the wrong foot.

"Let me help you with that." Justin passed me the books, grabbed the ten-pound bag of flour, and settled it on the trolley. "You can come take a look if you've got time."

I glanced at the open kitchen door. Chef Heston would yell at me if he caught me sneaking off, but I really did want to take a peek. "That would be great."

He took back the books. "Then follow me."

I walked alongside Justin, keeping an eye on the kitchen door to make sure I wasn't spotted. "Are things getting back to normal at work?"

His mouth twisted to the side. "Define normal?"

"You don't feel weird about working there after what happened to Bluebell?"

"Oh, yeah. I feel super weird. Although things are smoother now she's gone."

"You didn't like her?"

Justin shrugged. "I didn't hate her. She could be mean, though. Bluebell was always yelling at me. It's nice to work in a place where I'm not worried about someone shouting at me. Although now we have Herbert to deal with. He's not been the same since Bluebell died."

"I noticed he's not taken her death well. Were they close?"

"Not as close as he'd have liked them to be. Herbert was always staring at Bluebell. It was weird. She pretended not to notice most of the time, but she threw a tool at him once, and told him to get lost, so I guess she figured things out. She was pretty, but way too scary."

"Did Herbert ever talk to you about his interest in Bluebell?"

"Nah! I kept my head down and focused on the work. It was the safest thing to do. Sara said it wasn't any of our business. I always listen to her when it comes to relationships."

"You sound like the perfect guy." I grinned at him.

He chuckled. "I try. I usually fail."

"How much longer do you think you'll be working here?"

"I'm not sure. After Bluebell was killed, I thought about quitting."

"I understand why it must be odd to stay. But wouldn't you miss the work?"

"Yes! These kinds of jobs are hard to come by. Sara convinced me to stay. I don't want to let her down." He glanced at me.

"You still want to leave?"

"No. I don't know. You're going to think I'm crazy, but I keep looking at the spot where Bluebell was found. It gives me the chills. And I'm not into ghosts, but it seems colder in the old gallery since she died."

I raised my eyebrows. "You think Bluebell's ghost is haunting the place?"

He chuckled again. "I've never seen anything freaky like that, and I've worked in plenty of old, creepy places, but it's got me wondering about the afterlife. And if someone did kill her, she could be back for revenge."

I shuddered as we reached the old gallery. Maybe I didn't want to go inside, after all. I took a deep breath and followed Justin. The place was empty, and it did feel on the wrong side of chilly.

I checked in the gloomy corners but saw no signs of ghosts. "Other than the coldness, has anything else happened to make you think something odd is going on?"

Justin set down the books and opened a laptop in front of him. "It's probably me being forgetful, but I keep losing things. I put down a tool and then can't find it. Sara's always telling me I can't see for looking, but I'm sure I'm not that scatter brained."

I looked around the circular room again. A haunting in the east turret. If Lady Philippa found out about this, she'd be thrilled. It would be another ghost to add to her collection.

"Let me get the pictures up to show you what we've been working on."

He pulled up some pictures and zoomed in on different sections. "You see, the colors are becoming more vivid."

I peered at the screen which displayed dull yellow and blue splodges. "It'll look amazing when you're done."

"That's if we get it done," Justin said. "There's talk the funding may be pulled. Herbert mentioned it yesterday."

"I'm sorry to hear that. I suppose the funders are unhappy about the bad publicity Bluebell's death could generate."

"Not if you listen to Greta. She keeps saying it's an opportunity and we should push it for all it's worth. Herbert's not happy about that. He doesn't want his project linked to a murder. I don't much like the idea either." He looked at an open book by the side of the computer and then closed it. "I love this restoration work. Even though the place is a bit creepy, I don't want it to end."

"If the killer is found soon, you can still carry on. The press will move on to another story."

"Yeah, I hope so. I sort of wish it was an accident and the police have made a mistake. It would be easier to deal with."

"Did you see anything that night that made you suspicious of anyone? Anything you can think of could help to solve this quicker. Then you can focus on the work."

"Not really. I mean, I wasn't paying much attention that evening. I was tired, and we'd been working overtime. And I was starving. I kept pestering Sara to leave. She was angry at me because I forgot to get food in. She made me stay late to punish me for being so forgetful." He shrugged. "I am. I admit it. But leaving a guy hungry is cruel."

I smiled at him. "If you ever get desperate, you can come to the kitchen. There's always someone around who'll make you food. Although don't ask our head chef. He can be grumpy if you catch him on a bad day."

"Thanks. I'll take you up on that offer. Neither of us are great cooks. Anyway, I finally persuaded Sara to leave. We invited Herbert along, too. That guy lives off ready meals and tinned tuna, but he said he was busy. We left him and Bluebell and went back to the apartment."

"Was that typical for them both to stay working late?"

"Yeah. I didn't think anything of it."

"Was Herbert behaving strangely that night?"

Justin ran a hand through his hair. "He's always a bit strange. You get used to it. I guess he seemed tenser than usual. He'd had a row with Bluebell earlier in the day. There was something going on between them, but it wasn't my job to ask questions. And I didn't know Bluebell all that well. I don't consider myself stupid, and I know plenty about restoration, but Bluebell was like an encyclopedia. She knew everything."

"You kept out of her way?"

"Whenever I could. Sara was lucky. She could get away from her by working up on the scaffolding. We can only go up there one at a time." He glanced at the top of the scaffolding and shook his head. "She's way braver than me."

"It must help that you've got Sara here," I said.

"Yeah, she's great. I mean, it's a new relationship, but she's fun to be around. And she's my bodyguard when Greta gets too mean. It's kind of embarrassing that she's always taking care of me."

A car door slammed, and Justin hurried to the window. He peered out and groaned. "That's just what we need, the suit turning up. I didn't think he'd be here so soon."

I joined him by the window and looked out. A sleek silver sports car sat outside. "Who does that belong to?"

"Solomon King." Justin turned and shook his head. "The guy cares nothing for history. To him, this is a moneymaking venture and a way to schmooze the rich clients who give him their funds to invest. It's his firm that's involved with funding this project. Greta will be here in a minute to sweet talk him. I don't want to be around when she arrives." He hurried over to the workstation and grabbed his pile of books.

"This is the guy thinking of pulling the funding from the project?"

Justin nodded. "He's a rich jerk."

"Maybe you could convince him to keep supporting the restoration. Show him how important it is."

He gestured to a hole in his sweater. "A guy like that will pay zero attention to me. Unless I'm handing him a bag of cash, he'll stomp all over me. I'm out of here. You should go, too. I don't think Greta likes you much. But then she doesn't like anyone." He raced away before I could say goodbye.

A few seconds later, Greta's voice rang out a greeting to Solomon.

They stood talking outside, so I took another quick look at the pictures on the laptop. I compared them to the artist's impression left on the table. This place would be stunning when it was completed. There'd be cupids cavorting across the ceiling among fluffy white clouds and yellow flowers.

I grabbed up a book Justin had left behind from his pile. I hurried after him to give it back, when my ankle gave a warning twinge not to push too hard.

I slowed and looked at the book's title: *Audley Castle Myths and Legends*. I opened the title page and had a read. It sounded like an interesting bedtime book. If I didn't see Justin today to give it back, I'd have a browse through it and see what I could learn about the castle's legends.

I'd just reached the doorway when I heard giggling. I peeked round the corner, and my mouth dropped open. Solomon had Greta pinned against the wall and was whispering in her ear. Then he snuck a kiss on her.

Greta laughed, shook her head, and pushed him away. "You're terrible. We're working."

"You're always teasing me. I know you want me back."

"Solomon, what we had was fun, but it's over."

"Don't tell me you were just using me to get this project funded?" He pressed a hand to his heart.

"As if I'd need to do that. I'm a successful business woman. We enjoyed ourselves. Let's not spoil things."

He kissed her again. "I want more. You're a lot of fun to be around."

"Not here. I don't want to be gossiped about by the nosy staff."

"Where then? I have to see you."

She giggled again. "I'll think about it."

I ducked back as Greta pushed Solomon away.

"Let's go take a look at your project. I'll show you how I've been investing your money," she said.

I looked around, but there was nowhere to hide. I stepped back and pretended to be reading the book I held.

Greta appeared in the doorway. Beside her was Solomon, wearing a tailored pale gray suit. He had slicked back dark hair, a clean-shaven jaw, and sharp dark eyes.

"Oh! What are you doing in here?" Greta said.

I pulled my best surprised face. "Hi, Greta. Nothing interesting. Just seeing if the work crew needed anything to eat."

Her eyes narrowed, and she glanced at Solomon. "See what I told you about nosy staff."

He smirked at me.

Greta pursed her lips. "There's no one else in here. Get along. You're trespassing on an important project. I told the team we needed a private viewing this afternoon." She didn't bother to introduce me to Solomon, and simply strode past in her high heels. "This way."

Solomon glanced at me, but then looked away. My apron must have shown my place in the pecking order.

"Greta, before you go, have you got a moment?" I said.

"No." She kept on walking.

"Please. It's a personal matter."

She stopped walking and turned. "You don't know anything personal about me."

"I have a question about ..." I looked at Solomon. "It's a woman's thing."

Solomon shrugged. "I'll be over there." He pointed to the table and ambled away.

"What is it?" Greta marched back toward me.

"This will seem an odd thing to ask, but have you misplaced any underwear while you've been here?"

She glanced back at Solomon. "Why would I have any reason to remove my underwear while I was working?"

I suppressed a smile as her cheeks grew pink. "Some women carry around spares in their purses. It's just that I found some expensive knickers in here. I thought the owner would be missing them. They're from Chantelle's Secrets. Is that a brand you buy?"

Her eyes narrowed. "No. And why do you care about what brand of underwear I own?"

"I don't. You could wear giant granny pants with holes in for all I care. I was curious about why they were in here."

"You found them in the old gallery?"

"Yes. Well, my dog did. Two pairs. They're definitely not yours?"

She shook her head. "I can only think of one person they may belong to, and she's dead."

"Bluebell?"

"Yes. She always insisted on the best of everything. It went with her grand ambitions to claw her way to the top. She dressed for the job she wanted, not the one she had. Now you're wasting my time. Scram." Greta waved a hand at me.

I couldn't resist giving a little curtesy behind her back when she strutted away, before walking out of the old gallery.

My meeting with Justin and Greta had been useful. He'd confirmed his alibi, and Sara's, and highlighted the problem between Herbert and Bluebell. Everything was lining Herbert up as the prime suspect.

I looked back at the old gallery. I couldn't discount Greta, not just yet. She'd helped me solve the mystery of the underwear, but was Greta's desire for publicity and notoriety for this project making her deadly?

I had to consider her lack of alibi and her cold-hearted motives before I focused only on Herbert and his rejected love.

This mystery wasn't over yet.

Chapter 13

I headed back to the library with Meatball after work that day and tapped on the door. I hoped to find Alice and see if I could figure out what was going on with her.

The library was empty. The desk Alice had been working at was also cleared. All the books that had been scattered around her were gone.

"We may as well make use of the place while we're here, Meatball." I snuggled on a comfortable couch covered in soft downy cushions and tucked my feet underneath me. I placed a blanket next to me, so Meatball could hop up and join me.

I'd brought along the book Justin had left behind in the old gallery, and it didn't take many minutes before I was absorbed in the pages. The castle had a long and fascinating history, full of scandal and intrigue. There were even a few murders in its distant past. Some things never changed.

I'd just turned to the section on the castle's gardens, when a dull thud against one wall in the library made me jump.

Meatball growled and leaped off the couch. He trotted to the wall and sniffed it.

I slid from the couch and walked over to where the noise had come from.

Meatball was still growling softly as he examined the wall.

I ran my hand over it, then tapped several of the wooden panels. Priest passages ran throughout the castle. They'd been used hundreds of years ago to hide members of a religious order when under threat by King Henry the Eighth. There was most likely one behind this wall, but I had no clue how to get it open. And I wasn't sure I wanted to. Who would be sneaking around in the priest passages in the gloom?

Meatball scratched at the wall, trying to help me find the opening.

"Is someone behind there?" I whispered. "You don't think we're being snooped on by a ghost, do you?"

Meatball continued to growl, and the fur on the back of his neck rose.

Another thump had me jumping away. The lights overhead flickered, and I shivered as the temperature dropped. I'd meant the ghost comment as a joke. Now, I wasn't so sure.

Meatball whined and backed away, bumping into my legs.

"It's okay. It's nothing to be scared of. Probably. These old places always have bumps and creaks going on. It's just a pipe expanding."

His ears and tail lowered, suggesting he didn't believe me. I wasn't sure I believed me, either.

I crept back to the wall. The ends of my fingers were growing numb as the temperature sunk to uncomfortably chilly.

I'd just reached the paneling, when the lights went out and I was plunged into darkness.

I squeaked as there was another crash. Something heavy and soft landed against me. I lost my balance, tripped over and fell, bumping my head on the floor.

The lights flicked back on.

"Oh! Rupert. What are you doing?" I stared up at him as he pinned me to the floor with his body weight.

"Holly! I didn't know you were in here." He rolled off me and staggered to his feet. "I didn't mean to fall on you. I didn't hurt you, did I?"

"No, I'm fine." I took his hand, and he helped me to stand. "Was that you bashing around in the walls?"

"Yes! I've been exploring the priest passages. I didn't mean to scare you."

"You gave us both a fright. I thought one of Lady Philippa's ghosts was coming after us."

"Sorry. And sorry to Meatball." Rupert petted his head. "I heard someone walking around in the priest passage near my bedroom. I figured it was Alice. She's always using the tunnels to get about when she's doing something she shouldn't."

The room no longer felt so cold. It must have been my imagination playing tricks on me. "What's Alice up to? I came in here yesterday, and she snapped my head off and shoved me out of the room."

"You know what my sister's like. She's always doing something weird. Although she's being particularly odd at the moment. I've barely seen her. If she's not in here, she's locked away in her bedroom. She had a sign on the door earlier today saying do not disturb."

"Did you see Alice when you were in the priest passages?"

"No. And I snuck a look in her room when I was passing along the passage. She's up there. It wasn't her walking around. That's why I decided to keep looking, to make sure no one was up to mischief. Then I got myself turned around and wasn't sure where I was. I was fumbling to find a way out." He looked around the room. "Why were you in the dark when I came into the library?"

I glanced at the lit ceiling light. "The light blinked out all of a sudden."

"It must be the dodgy wiring again," Rupert said.

It had to be a wiring problem. Ghosts couldn't turn off light switches. "Do you want me to help you look for whoever is making the noises? I'm happy to, so long as we're not chasing after a ghost."

He grinned. "It's only granny who believes in the castle ghosts. I just wanted to make sure we didn't have an intruder in the castle."

"Should we call in security? After all, there is a killer on the loose."

"Not many people know about the priest passages," Rupert said. "It has to be someone in the family, or a member of security snooping around."

"Or it really could be one of your granny's ghosts."

"There's a thought. It could be Granny. She's been troubled by something lately. I went to see her earlier today, and she was barely making any sense. She kept talking about a bowl that had gone missing. She said she had to find it. And she isn't sleeping because of her bad dreams. Maybe she's finally lost her marbles and is wandering around lost in the priest passages."

"If that's the case, we should go in and get her out," I said. "Let's take a look in the passages, to make sure it isn't her. I'd hate to think she was scared and on her own."

"Of course. Let's go and see if my granny is misbehaving."

I crept in behind Rupert, Meatball sticking close to my ankles, and into a narrow, gray stone passage.

I shuffled along close behind Rupert, jumping at every small sound. "What kind of noises did you hear?"

"Footsteps and thudding," he said.

"That's what I heard in the library, but after you fell on me, I figured it was you."

"It could have been me. I was fumbling around for ages trying to find the latch to get out. Most of the doors don't have them. The poor priests would get stuck for days. Some never got out. We even had to clear a few bones we discovered about ten years ago. Those poor souls never got free."

"Bones!" I shuddered and grabbed the back of Rupert's jacket to make sure I kept him close.

Meatball nudged past, getting bolder. He trotted ahead of us, sniffing the stone floor.

"That's it, Meatball. You find the intruder," Rupert said.

I bumped into Rupert when he abruptly halted. "What is it? Did you hear something?"

"No. I thought I saw a mouse."

"I don't mind mice. Do you want me to lead?"

"No, you stay where you are. But you can deal with the rodents, and I'll deal with the ghosts."

We walked along in silence for a few moments, stopping every now and again to listen.

Meatball was sniffing around but didn't seem overly bothered by the gloom and the occasional cobweb. So far, there was no sign of ghosts, mice, or anyone else.

"How's the investigation going into Bluebell's murder?" Rupert whispered.

"Everything is pointing at Herbert, but I'm not certain about Greta. And I met Solomon King earlier today. I didn't think much of him. I wouldn't mind having a chat with him."

"I can help with that. My father wants me to take a more active role in the castle, and this is one of the projects he's given me to oversee. Although the fact there's been a murder whilst it's happening hasn't put me in his good books. He'll probably give me some boring task next, or send me away to business school. I can't think of anything duller."

I bit my bottom lip. Did Rupert know about the women his parents were setting him up with? Was that why they were doing it? They thought he needed a woman to make him more level headed and sensible? Rupert could be absent minded, but I'd always found that endearing.

I opened my mouth to ask him, but then snapped it shut. It wasn't my place to interrogate him about his love life. And his parents wouldn't keep something so important a secret from him. Not when it would affect the rest of his life.

"If you could get me an introduction to Solomon that would be great," I said. "It's a long shot, but his company has money invested in the restoration work. I want to see what he thought about Bluebell. Do you know if they ever met?"

"Yes. Solomon visited a couple of times before we made the final arrangements. Bluebell was involved from the start. She came to a meeting to outline the work. Greta brought her along. I'll sort something out. I can fix up a lunch for tomorrow if you're free. I know Solomon's in the area, so it's a perfect opportunity to talk to him."

"Thanks. Campbell's still focusing on Herbert as the killer, but until there's evidence to link him to Bluebell's murder, we have to keep looking at the other suspects. Even if it's just to discount them."

"I'm no expert in the business of murder, but I've gotten to know Herbert since this project started," Rupert said. "I like him. I don't see him as a killer."

"No one does. But if he was obsessed with Bluebell, his unrequited love may have tipped him over the edge."

"Ah! We all know about that." Rupert's tone was wistful.

"Are you in love with someone?" I said.

He was silent for a long time as we continued to explore the passages. "I imagine what it must be like, to be fond of someone and for them to feel differently about you. Have you got experience of that?"

"I, um, maybe. Have you spoken to this person you like?"

"Yes. We speak all the time. But it's ... difficult." He turned so fast that I ran straight into his chest.

Rupert caught hold of my shoulders. "Do you understand what I'm saying, Holly?"

I looked up at him in the gloom. "I ... I think so. Sometimes it's not as simple as two people liking each other. It should be. Nothing else should matter, but I understand that's not always the case. Especially not for someone who'll be in charge of a huge castle one day."

He let out a soft sigh. "That's true. I wish it was easy. Then Alice would finally get together with Campbell and stop mooning over him. She's like a teenage girl with a crush."

"You know she likes him?"

"She has eyes for Campbell and no one else. My parents have been trying to find a suitable match for Alice for a while. I think they've almost given up. I'm worried they're going to focus on me next."

So he didn't know about the matchmaking his parents were planning for him. Should I tell him the truth? He needed warning, so he could be prepared.

"Rupert, there's something—"

Meatball barked and raced ahead of us.

"That was a thud. Quick! Follow me." Rupert grabbed my hand and tugged me along the corridor.

We rounded the corner, and he slowed.

"Is anyone there?" I peered over his shoulder.

"We're too late. I really am beginning to think it could be the ghosts snooping on us. No one else can move that quickly. And it's not Alice playing games with me. She's too clumsy to sneak around like this. And she'd only start laughing and give herself away."

Meatball trotted back into view.

"Did our sneaky person escape you, too?" I said to him.

He sniffed the floor, getting his nose covered in dust, and gave an enormous sneeze.

"That's blown our cover," Rupert said. "Not that we need a reason to hide. Perhaps we should go back to the library. It's getting late. And I didn't mean to disturb you."

I turned, pleased to see we were still holding hands. "It's fine. I was just doing some reading."

We made our way slowly back to the library, and after some fumbling around, discovered the latch to open the door that led into the room.

Rupert walked me over to the couch and picked up the book I'd dropped. He flipped over the pages and smiled. "You're learning about the castle's history. Don't believe all these legends and myths. If half the treasures they say were hidden actually existed, I'd be able to buy another five castles and have plenty of change left over." He handed me the book. "I'll fix a lunch for tomorrow with Solomon. Any time suit you?"

"Whenever you can make it. Just let me know. I'll be there."

He stepped closer. His gaze went to my mouth.

I tensed. Was Rupert going to kiss me?

"You're a good person, Holly. You always look out for other people. I hope you're always around to look out for me. Your kindness is something I never want to lose." He kissed my cheek softly, then stepped back.

"Oh! Sure. I'll always be here. I'm not planning on going anywhere."

"That's the best news I've heard all day. Well, good night."

I stared at him as he left the library. What was I going to do about Rupert? As his friend, I should have told him what I knew about the upcoming matchmaking activities planned for him, but how would that help us? We couldn't be together. His parents would insist he marry someone suitable.

I shook my head. There wasn't even an us. I was being ridiculous.

"Any suggestions, library ghosts?" I looked around, but no one replied. "Figured as much."

Meatball whined and nudged my leg with his head.

"I agree. Enough talking to thin air." I tucked the book under my arm. "Come on, Meatball. It's time for bed."

Chapter 14

"This is an excellent choice of wine, Lord Rupert."

I stood outside the dining room, checking I didn't have any flour on my clothes, when I heard Solomon King.

"We have a big wine cellar here," Rupert said. "There's always plenty of choice."

"I imagine you do. I have my own small collection. I enjoy the rarer vintages," Solomon said.

I did a quick check of my appearance in the large gold-framed mirror by the entrance to the dining room, smoothed my hands over my hair, and then entered the room.

Rupert turned and smiled at me. "Holly, there you are. I was worried you weren't going to show."

"Who is this?" Solomon said.

"Solomon King, I'd like you to meet Holly Holmes. She's an integral part of the castle," Rupert said.

I shook hands with Solomon. "It's nice to meet you."

His gaze ran over me. "I've seen you somewhere before."

"Yes. Yesterday in the old gallery. I was there when Greta was showing you around."

His dark eyes narrowed a fraction. "Of course. So what do you do for the Audley family that's so integral?"

"Holly stops us from starving," Rupert said.

"I'm not sure I understand," Solomon said.

"Having excellent food is an integral part of my life," Rupert said. "Holly's the best baker we've ever employed in the castle."

Solomon lifted his groomed eyebrows. "She works in your kitchens?"

"And she does an outstanding job," Rupert said. "I expect we'll get to sample her treats later."

A wicked gleam entered Solomon's eyes. "How delightful."

"Shall we take a seat at the table?" Rupert gestured toward the food that had been laid out. "I thought we'd keep things casual. We can serve ourselves."

Solomon took another sip of his wine before nodding. "Why not? Let's sample some of Miss Holmes' treats."

"I didn't make any of this." I ignored the innuendo as I settled in the seat Rupert had pulled out for me. "I tend to stick to the desserts. It's what I'm best at."

Solomon set down his wine glass. "I'm curious as to why you're here. I understand you satisfy Rupert's … sweet tooth, but is it normal for a baker to dine with the family?"

"It is unusual," I said. "The Audleys are a kind and generous family to work for."

"We wouldn't have it any other way," Rupert said. "Holly helps to make the castle a home."

"You're too kind," I said.

"Yes, he is." Solomon flapped his napkin over one knee and helped himself to some smoked salmon. "I hope you're not taking advantage of that generosity, Holly."

"I wouldn't do that," I said. My dislike of Solomon grew every time he opened his mouth.

"Of course not," Rupert said. "Holly's not like that."

"When you get money and influence, you need to be careful who you let into your inner circle," Solomon said. "Of course, we don't have the same level of wealth, but I'm always cautious about new friendships. The other person always wants something out of the relationship. It usually involves me parting with cash."

"Lord Rupert invited me here because I have an interest in history," I said. "Especially the project you're supporting in the old gallery."

"Holly studied history at university," Rupert said. "She wants to know all about the restoration work."

Solomon's forehead wrinkled. "I can't tell you much about the actual project. We just supply the funding. The historians can be found grubbing about up on that scaffolding if you need to know the details."

"But you're happy with how the project's going?" I said.

"It could go faster. The recent delays have bloated the budget," Solomon said.

"Bluebell Brewster's murder, you mean?"

"Exactly that. Greta has convinced me that everything's under control, but we need to be careful."

"What do you need to be careful about?" Rupert said.

"We need to make sure attention isn't taken from the reason we're supporting this project," Solomon said.

"To widen public interest in historical preservation work?" I said.

Solomon shrugged. "Of course, that has its place. But we also need to ensure people know that Viking Investments isn't all about capitalism. When you make a lot of money, people get spiteful. They point the finger and make unfounded accusations. It's bad for business."

"I'm sure people have forgotten about that little incident from a few years back," Rupert said.

"What's this?" I said.

"It's nothing," Solomon said swiftly. "It's in the past. And this community funding is something we've been planning for a long time." He grabbed the wine bottle and topped up his glass. "Anyone else need a refill?"

I waved away his offer. "I've missed something."

"Viking Investment set up a community foundation after one of the company directors was found to have ... how was it described, Solomon?" There was a twinkle of amusement in Rupert's eyes as he ate his salmon.

Solomon glowered at him. "The director made a mistake. He was incorrectly filing his expenses."

"To the tune of half a million," Rupert said.

I almost choked on my food. "That's a huge mistake."

"The guy never had a great head for figures," Solomon said. "He's no longer involved in the leadership of the company. But we've had to do a lot of damage control."

"Plus, you think it's important to support the communities you work in," Rupert said.

Solomon forced a smile. "Of course. That too."

I took a sip from my water glass. It all fitted into place. Viking Investments had zero interest in assisting with art restoration projects. They were only involved to clear up their sordid reputation.

"How long will you be staying in Audley St. Mary?" Rupert asked.

"I should be here a couple more days. My boss has asked me to keep an eye on this project, considering what's happened. We need to make sure we can pick up the slack."

"They'd welcome volunteer help if you're offering," I said.

Solomon snorted a laugh. "I'm simply here to crack the whip and stop Herbert mooning about, so he gets on with things."

"He's finding it hard since Bluebell died," I said. "Did you know her well?"

Solomon glanced at me. "No. We only met a couple of times."

Rupert shook his head. "Everyone here is still shocked by what happened."

"I imagine you are," Solomon said. "You won't have murders happening around a sleepy little place like this too often."

"You'd be surprised," I muttered. "Did you visit the castle on the day of Bluebell's murder? Perhaps you saw something that could be useful to the police."

"I did drop by that day. I was in the area and thought I'd see how things were going. And I wanted to check some information with Greta. I didn't stay for long."

"Did you get a chance to explore the village? It's beautiful around here," I said.

"Not really. It's too quiet for my liking. I had dinner at the pub while I caught up on my emails, then I headed into Cambridge." Solomon drank more wine. "How close are the police to tidying everything up?"

"They're still investigating," Rupert said. "We also have our castle security team working on it. We hire ex-forces and former police officers to guard the family. They're excellent at their jobs."

"That makes sense. I had some guy demanding answers from me the other day. It felt like a military interrogation. I had nothing useful to tell him," Solomon said.

"That was probably Campbell Milligan," Rupert said. "He's head of security at the castle."

"That's the name he gave. I told him he needed to ask Herbert what he was doing with Bluebell. The guy had a real thing for her, but she was way out of his league. She was more my type when she tidied herself up. Pretty in an arrogant sort of way. But he liked her."

"Herbert told you that?" I said.

"He didn't have to say a word. It was so obvious. And I got the impression Herbert doesn't have much experience with women. He stammered every time Bluebell was around and kept praising her work. It was pathetic. If he was into her, he needed to man up and prove he was in charge. She may have respected him more. As it was, I got the impression she felt sorry for him."

"Everyone on this project seems to be romantically involved with a colleague," I said.

"What do you mean?"

"Herbert and Bluebell. Sara and Justin. You and Greta. Have you been dating for long?" I asked.

Solomon took a gulp of wine. "We're not dating. What makes you say that?"

I glanced at Rupert and raised my eyebrows. "Oh, my mistake. You seemed to know each other well. I figured you were in a relationship."

Solomon carefully placed down his fork and fixed me with a sharp look. "This project is purely business."

"Aren't you engaged to someone?" Rupert said.

"That's right." Solomon glared at me one more time before turning his attention to Rupert. "I recently proposed to my childhood sweetheart. She's a doll. She knew me before I joined Viking Investments, so I know she's not trying to get my money by marrying me. It's so difficult to know who to trust when you're dating. You must know all about that, Lord Rupert. As soon as women know who you are, they get that predatory gleam in their eyes and start asking for gifts and vacations."

Rupert tugged at his shirt collar. "That's not been too much of a problem so far."

Solomon smirked at me. "You need to be careful who you trust. There'll always be someone scheming to take things from you. That's why I got engaged to Katie. She's sweet, pretty, uncomplicated, and kept busy by her teaching job. I'm free to come and go as I like, do my work, enjoy myself, and not worry about my assets. Plus, she adores me."

"She's a lucky lady." The woman must need her head examined.

"She sure is." Solomon picked up his fork. "So, you see, Holly, I couldn't be involved with Greta. Unless you're suggesting I'm cheating on my fiancée."

"I can't imagine you'd do such a thing. Not when Katie sounds so nice." I pasted a smile on my face.

Solomon nodded and kept on eating. He looked at Rupert. "When this Bluebell business has been sorted, we'll plan some publicity events. My boss is considering hosting an international conference for investment bankers. The old gallery would be a great place to show off to them."

"I'm sure we can come to some arrangement," Rupert said. "Although the old gallery will eventually be open for public viewing. It's the reason we wanted your support, so we could make the area as accessible as possible."

"Of course. But I've already cleared everything with your father. He's a good man. Very amenable to the idea of corporate investment. Old places like this always need extra capital. This castle is nice to look at, but it must cost a fortune to run. I'm sure you're good for the cash, but it helps when you can get extra finance in place." Solomon sipped his wine.

Rupert's expression hardened. "I assure you, we have plenty of money if we wanted to do the renovation work ourselves."

Solomon raised a hand. "I'm not saying you don't. But why spend your money when you can have ours?"

Rupert took a big bite of food and thumped down his knife.

The next few moments were spent in an awkward silence. I didn't believe a word of what Solomon said. He'd flirted with Greta, and she'd returned his interest. And it sounded like he'd only gotten engaged to his fiancée so he wouldn't fall prey to some money grubber who wanted his assets.

Solomon's phone rang. He pulled it out of his pocket and checked the caller. "I need to take this. It's an investment client. I could be awhile. Don't start on the after-lunch brandies without me." He stood and hurried away, his phone by his ear.

"What did you make of that?" Rupert said. "I don't like him."

"He's not my favorite person," I said. "And he wasn't being truthful about Greta. I saw them together. They didn't realize I was there, but they were being intimate with each other. Solomon kissed Greta."

"I don't know Solomon well, but I know his reputation. I did background checks before we agreed to this private investment. He's a playboy. He likes the social scene in London. And although he's discreet, there are rumors his fiancée isn't the only woman he's close to."

"And his interest in the castle is all about money and reputation saving."

Rupert frowned and sat back in his seat. "I'm beginning to regret getting Viking Investments involved in this project. It was my father's suggestion. He wants to divert some money from the castle and build a new estate."

"I didn't know that," I said. "You're planning to expand in Audley St. Mary?"

"No, not locally, but possibly abroad. He's not certain yet." Rupert glanced away. "Father's mentioned several times that he'd like me to run this new estate."

"You're leaving Audley Castle?" My heart sank. There'd be no more Rupert ambling around the castle grounds, eating my cake and making me think about a happy ending with him that would never happen. The place wouldn't be the same without him.

"It's not definite. I've made no decision about whether I'll run this new estate. But Father seems eager for me to be involved, and I don't like to disappoint him."

"Of course not. It's a shame you don't see much of him. He doesn't come here often."

"He hates the cold winters. And with homes in Antigua, Italy, and Dubai, he has little reason to come back."

"You and Alice are great reasons to visit all the time."

He smiled. "Yes, I suppose we are. Anyway, it's time I found a purpose, that's what he keeps telling me. It'll stop me from drifting around this place and getting in everyone's way."

"This place is your home. You love it here, don't you?"

His gaze settled on me. "Yes, I do love it."

I focused on my napkin, folding it over several times. "We need to consider Solomon as a suspect in Bluebell's murder. He pretty much dismissed her as nothing more than an attractive plaything, and an inconvenience after she died. But maybe she was causing him problems. This project is all about money and prestige for him."

"And reputation saving."

"Yes. That, too."

"And he was in the area on the day Bluebell died."

"So he had an opportunity to get to Bluebell."

"But Solomon freely admitted to the visit. If he wanted to conceal his movements, why be so quick to share?" Rupert said.

"He couldn't have hidden it. We'd have found out," I said.

Rupert stabbed at the remaining food on his plate. "Why would he murder Bluebell?"

"She may have insisted the company invest more into the restoration work. I can't imagine Solomon likes being told what to do."

"Viking Investments has plenty of spare money."

"Maybe. But Solomon decides how it gets spent, not the project he's funding. And Bluebell was blunt. She wouldn't have stood for any of his nonsense. If he told her no, she'd have kept on hassling him."

"So she demanded more money, and he didn't like that? Is that something worth killing over?"

I tapped my fingers on the table as I considered the motives. "Bluebell could have found out he was seeing Greta and confronted him, maybe even suggested she might talk to others about it if he didn't fund the project. You saw his reaction when I mentioned his relationship with Greta."

"He wouldn't want that coming out."

"Solomon has a ruthless streak. It wouldn't surprise me if he invested in this project because of his interest in Greta. He wanted to get on her good side so he could get her into bed. He didn't realize how complicated and expensive this project would be. The bills started coming in, more money was demanded, and his boss began asking difficult questions that he couldn't answer."

"Solomon killed Bluebell to ruin the project? He figured if he killed her, Viking would pull their investment to avoid the bad press?"

"This is business for him. The little people don't matter. Solomon said everything was going well, but we need to find out if that's true."

"How do we do that?" Rupert said.

"Do you know his boss?" I glanced at the door. I could just hear Solomon on his phone, but couldn't make out the words.

"I do. Stephen Hatton. My father's had business dealings with him. We've met at several functions."

"You need to call him. Ask his honest opinion on how this project is going."

"What if it gets back to Solomon that we've been prying into his work?"

"You're entitled to pry. This is your home. You need to make sure you can trust the people coming into it. And ask about Solomon, too. See what Stephen thinks of him." I pulled out my phone and brought up the contact details of Viking Investments. "Are you up for doing this?"

Rupert grinned. "Of course. If it'll help the murder investigation, I'll give it a try."

I dialed the number and handed my phone to Rupert. Then I jumped up and headed to the door, easing it closed to make sure Solomon couldn't hear the conversation.

"Hello. I'd like to speak to Stephen Hatton." Rupert paused. "It's Lord Rupert Audley. Thank you."

Rupert had gone from sweet to masterful, his tone ringing with authority.

I remained by the door, my heart beating a little faster than usual. He was suddenly twice as handsome when he took charge.

He looked over at me and nodded. "I'm in. Come and listen."

I took a quick glance at the door, then hurried over.

Rupert lifted the phone away from his ear so I could hear the other side of the conversation. "Stephen. It's Rupert Audley."

"Lord Rupert, what a pleasure. How is life in Audley St. Mary?" a posh, booming voice said.

"It couldn't be better. I wanted to check in with the restoration project. Everything good at your end?"

"It's funny you've made contact now. I was just thinking about the castle. I have the latest report on my desk. I was planning on reading it this afternoon."

"Do you have any concerns I should know about?" Rupert said.

There was a pause, then Stephen cleared his throat. "I'll come clean with you. There have been some issues raised among our board members."

"Because of the incident with Bluebell Brewster?"

"Yes. Of course, that was a terrible tragedy. But our PR person is putting a spin on things."

"What kind of a spin? How can you make a murder positive?" Rupert said.

"She's suggesting a haunted castle event once all the unpleasant murder business has been dealt with. I'm sure she's mentioned it to you. Greta's excellent at fighting fires like this."

"No, it's the first I've heard about it. Don't you think it's disrespectful? A woman was killed in the old gallery. It's not entertainment."

"Ah! Yes, it's a sensitive topic. But it could give you a beneficial boost to visitor numbers. People love all that ghost rubbish," Stephen said. "No one's been arrested yet, have they?"

"Not yet. But it's only a matter of time," Rupert said. "However, we won't have any tawdry events that manipulate this tragedy."

There was silence for several seconds. "Of course. Whatever you think, Lord Rupert. I have to say, with the increasing costs of the project and the murder of this woman, I'm considering ending things early. The painting restoration looks almost finished, anyway. You must be pleased with our investment."

I gestured for Rupert to mute his phone. "That's not true. There are weeks of work still to be done."

He nodded and unmuted his phone. "It's a shame if you go that route. Does Solomon King know about the plans to withdraw funding?"

"I've had several conversations with him about it. He should be down your way right now if you want to tie up the final arrangements."

"He is here," Rupert said. "But he's busy with another client. I just wanted to make sure everything was running smoothly from your end."

"I'll have a word with him about that. Solomon is a great guy, dedicated to his work, but he can get distracted."

"Mention Greta," I whispered.

Rupert looked confused.

"See if you can find out if they're involved."

He nodded. "Of course. I imagine that's especially true if there's a pretty woman around. We were just having lunch, and Solomon mentioned being interested in someone he works with. I think her name is Greta."

Stephen roared a laugh. "No doubt. Solomon is a rogue. And I'm sure you've met Greta. The first time I did, she intimidated the heck out of me, but I had to have her on my team. She can always put the right spin on any publicity blip. And she's not bad to look at."

"I've met Miss Davies. I'm glad she's an asset to your company."

"Solomon and Greta make a great team. You have our best people working with you. I'll make sure Solomon keeps you informed about what's going on. I hope it won't be a problem if we do end things early? No hard feelings."

"Not at all," Rupert said. "Sometimes relationships don't work out."

"I knew you'd see sense. You're like your father. You have a head for business."

Rupert grimaced. "Thank you for your time." He ended the call and turned to me. "Solomon lied to us again. He knew the project was going sideways and kept quiet about it."

"He did. And it sounds like it's under pressure to close early," I said. "If Solomon lied about this, what else has he lied about?"

"His relationship with Greta?"

"Most definitely. And possibly his alibi on the night of Bluebell's murder. We've just found ourselves another suspect."

Chapter 15

After my lunch with Solomon and Rupert, I had to rush back to work. Chef Heston was particularly snippy all afternoon, no doubt because he knew I'd had lunch with Rupert. He gave me all the boring jobs and insisted I stay late to clean off the baking trays before putting them in the dishwasher.

Meatball was bouncing around outside as I emerged from the kitchen. He spun in a circle and raced away, keen to get some exercise.

"Sorry, I didn't mean to keep you waiting. Let's give you a nice long run." I winced as my ankle twinged. I'd been on my feet most of the day, and the last thing my sore foot needed was a long walk. But I couldn't neglect Meatball. And he was happy racing about without me keeping up with him.

Something small and hard pinged off the back of my head.

I spun round to discover a tennis ball by my feet.

Campbell was in the distance, strolling toward me, an amused look on his face.

I bent down and picked up the tennis ball. "Did you throw this at me?"

He grinned as he got nearer. "My mistake. I meant to throw it for Meatball."

I rubbed the back of my head. There was no way his aim could have been that off. I threw the ball at him. Campbell caught it with ease.

Meatball raced back, having spotted the tennis ball. He launched himself at Campbell, his tail wagging furiously.

Campbell lobbed the tennis ball, and Meatball charged after it.

"While we're on the subject of balls," I said, "why is my face on the stress ball you loaned me?"

His grin widened. "You've lost me."

I thumped his arm. "You did put my face on it. Gran said it was me."

Campbell lifted one shoulder. "You stress me out. That ball helps take the edge off."

"Unbelievable."

"We do what we have to, to get by in this crazy place."

"But it's my face."

"I know. I see it poking into my security business most days."

"Only about once a month."

"That's more than enough." He slid a glare my way. "I hear you had lunch with Solomon King today."

"Now who's poking into private business?"

"This isn't private. Not when Lord Rupert is involved."

"I asked him to organize it."

"And were you going to tell me about your meeting?"

"Of course. Just like you tell me everything."

He grunted. "I see you're still limping."

"I am. But my ankle is getting better."

"It would be healed by now if you properly rested it. See what happens when you don't follow orders."

"I have rested it." I shook my head at him. "Do you want to hear how my lunch went?"

"Sure. But why are you focusing on Solomon? Do you have something on him to make him a suspect?"

"I have a bad feeling about him."

"You and your feelings."

"It's called a gut instinct. It's effective. I see cops use it all the time on TV shows."

"Sure. On TV shows that aren't real. It's also called being nosy."

"Which means you aren't interested in learning what I found out?"

He sighed. "Go on. What did you learn about Solomon?"

Meatball returned the ball to Campbell, and he threw it for him again.

"The restoration project funding is at risk. Solomon claimed everything was going well, but when Rupert spoke to his boss—"

"You got Lord Rupert involved in this gut feeling of yours?"

"It was a phone call. He was safe. There was zero risk. I encouraged him to make the call to see if Solomon was being truthful about how the project was going. It turns out, Solomon's boss isn't happy. It's likely the money will be withdrawn, and the project will end early. He claimed it was getting too expensive, and Bluebell's murder was making his trustees nervous."

"That's not really a surprise. Who'd want to fund a project where someone's been killed?"

"But Solomon lied to us. He said everything was going smoothly."

"To save face in front of Lord Rupert."

"Maybe. He also lied about his relationship with Greta. I saw them together. They're more than colleagues. And Solomon is engaged to another woman."

"He wouldn't be the first man to cheat."

"Are you a cheater?"

"No. I take my responsibilities seriously. So you caught Solomon out on a couple of lies. That doesn't make him a killer."

"It makes him untrustworthy. And he was in the area the night of Bluebell's murder. Rupert and I came up with several reasons as to why he'd want her dead."

"You mean you came up with wild theories, and Lord Rupert was too polite to tell you that you were being ridiculous?"

"I won't share my theories if you keep calling them ridiculous."

"Outlandish?"

"I'm about to walk away."

"How about preposterous?"

"I'm going now." I turned.

"Hold up. Tell me your theories." Campbell threw the ball for Meatball.

I huffed out a breath. "Very well. But I'm only staying because Meatball is having so much fun."

"Sure you are. So …"

"So, Bluebell learned the project was at risk. She confronted Solomon, demanded more money, and insisted the project stay open. I doubt he takes confrontation well. Or Bluebell could have tried to blackmail Solomon because she knew about his cheating. He'd have hated that."

"Okay, neither of those theories are that crazy."

"Thanks. And I just thought of another. What if Solomon's relationship with Greta had gone sideways, and he decided to mess things up for her? It sounds like she's got a good reputation at Viking Investments. Solomon wanted her gone, so decided to end her career."

"By killing someone? Wouldn't he have killed Greta, not Bluebell? That would have put a permanent stop to her career."

"It could have also brought their relationship into the spotlight. Solomon wouldn't have risked that."

Campbell shook his head. "What's his alibi?"

"He said he was in Cambridge. He had dinner at the local pub and was doing some work before that. But he could have snuck back to the castle. It's an easy drive."

Campbell was quiet for a moment. "We've checked the CCTV for that night. No cars came into the castle grounds that late."

"He could have parked in a lane and walked the rest of the way." I frowned. I couldn't picture Solomon trekking across a field to sneak in and kill someone. He wouldn't want to muddy up his designer suit.

"I'm still liking Herbert for this murder. He's got a strong motive and had plenty of opportunity to kill Bluebell."

I sighed. I didn't want it to be Herbert. I liked the guy.

Campbell shrugged. "I get your hesitation in pointing the finger at him. He's the most unlikely killer in the world, but everything suggests it was him."

"Herbert has no alibi, he had a crush on the victim, and he lied about liking her. He does seem the most obvious suspect. What are you going to do about it?"

"Finish this case."

"We're going to arrest Herbert?"

Campbell threw the ball for Meatball again. "No, you're not arresting anyone. I'll take him in for formal questioning when he gets back. I planned to do it earlier today, but he's gone off with Sara and Justin on a supplies trip."

"You don't think he's trying to escape?"

"I don't think he even realizes we're looking at him for Bluebell's murder. He's not a flight risk."

"It could have been an accident. Herbert didn't mean to kill her."

"This wasn't an accident. Bluebell was hunted down and killed. Herbert must have chased her up the scaffolding and shoved her off."

"But not deliberately. Maybe they argued. They got in a scuffle and Bluebell lost her balance. She could have fallen. Herbert may even have tried to save her."

"We'll find out the truth," Campbell said. "There's enough circumstantial evidence to make Herbert the prime suspect."

"I don't disagree, but he's fragile. Don't force a confession out of him."

Campbell shook his head. "I'm not a member of the Gestapo. I don't force anything out of anyone."

"What will you do to him?"

"I'll pull apart his alibi, set out his motive, the opportunity he had, and the evidence that he had feelings for Bluebell. If he is a decent guy who made a mistake, he'll tell the truth."

I nodded. "And working every day in the old gallery, the place where he murdered the woman he loved, must be affecting his mental health. I expect he'll be relieved to make a confession."

We walked along together for several minutes as Campbell continued to lob the ball for Meatball.

Something didn't feel right, even when Campbell set it all out and it made sense. Herbert was the obvious choice. But maybe he was too obvious.

"Do you want me to finish walking Meatball?" Campbell said.

I looked over at my furry best friend. He was having such a fun time with the tennis ball that it seemed cruel to make him go home early. "If you don't mind. You've got a good throwing arm."

"The best. And I have nothing else to do. I'm just waiting for a potential killer to come back to the castle. I'll drop Meatball off at the apartment later."

"Thanks, Campbell. Let me know how it goes with Herbert. And be gentle with him."

He arched an eyebrow. "You want me to be gentle with a killer?"

"You know what I mean. If Herbert did this, he must be feeling awful."

"Holly, you stick to the baking, and I'll stick to dealing with the killers." He walked away with Meatball.

I watched them play for a few minutes. I had mixed feelings about Herbert being questioned and charged with Bluebell's murder, but even the nicest of guys snapped if they got pushed too hard. And if it was him, he needed to pay for his crime.

❦

I jerked awake and lay still for a moment, holding my breath and trying to figure out what had woken me.

Meatball shuffled up to my head and licked my cheek.

"Did you hear a noise?" I whispered.

The light was still on by my bed. I looked around, but I was alone in the room. I peered over the edge of the bed and let out a relieved sigh. The book of Audley Castle myths and legends had fallen off the bed. I must have dozed off while reading it.

I leaned down and picked up the book before closing it and setting it on my bedside table.

I was about to turn off the light when my phone buzzed. I checked the display, surprised to see I'd four missed calls from Lady Philippa, and there were two text messages from her. She never used her cell phone unless it was an emergency.

I blinked the sleep out of my eyes and sat up. I opened the first message.

Danger. Ghosts say hell. Problem. Gallop horse.

I rubbed my eyes. Gallop horse? What did that mean?

"Is Lady Philippa sleep texting me?" I rubbed Meatball's head as I checked the next message. It was full of more garbled words that didn't make sense.

"I hope she's okay." I checked the time. It had just gone midnight.

I accessed my voice messages and listened to the first one.

There's trouble coming. You must get to the castle. Get help.

The next message was similar. *Holly, is that you? Oh! This is still your recorded voice. Pick up. Come at once.*

I flipped back my covers and stood. I headed to my window and peered out. I could see the east turret from my apartment, and there was a light burning in Lady Philippa's window.

I listened to the next message. *There's death coming to the castle. You must hurry.* She'd left this last message only a few minutes ago.

Dread trickled through me as I dashed out of the bedroom. I shoved my feet into my boots and grabbed my jacket and keys.

"Come on, Meatball. Lady Philippa needs us." I raced outside in my cupcake print pajamas and limp-ran toward the east turret.

I dialed Lady Philippa's number.

"Holly! At last. I thought something had happened to you."

"I was asleep. It's late. What's going on?"

"I had a premonition. Someone's about to die."

"Who? Where are they?"

"I keep seeing something bad happening to one of my ancestor's statues. His head will be used for something awful."

"A statue?" I slowed my pace. "This is an actual person we're talking about? Someone's really in danger?"

"Yes! The statue will be used to hit the victim. Holly, you must get to them."

"Who is it?"

"I don't know. It's not a family member."

"Has it happened yet?"

"I don't know that either. But it'll be soon. I woke up not long ago and felt sick. I was full of fear and felt the need to escape. I'm sure I'm sensing the victim's panic."

"I'll try to stop this happening, but I need to know where the murder will take place." I was twenty feet from the entrance to the east turret when there was a loud yell, and something smashed on the ground.

My breath caught in my throat. I stared hard at the intense blackness surrounding the entrance to the turret. It was the last place I wanted to go, but I had no choice. There was someone in there, and they were in trouble.

Lady Philippa gasped. "Holly, you're too late. I think it's happened. They're dead."

"I'm going to investigate. Hang up and call Campbell. Get him to come to the east turret."

"Campbell! Of course. Be careful, Holly."

"Stay in your room, Lady Philippa, while I see what's going on." I raced into the old gallery with Meatball.

Although it was dark, the curtains hadn't been drawn over the windows, and a full moon illuminated the scene in front of me. My breath stuck in my throat and I staggered back.

Herbert was lying on the floor.

Chapter 16

I squeaked, my shaking hand going to cover my mouth as my breathing grew shallow. I glanced around the old gallery at the dense, black shadows around us, before hurrying over to Herbert.

He was on his back, his eyes open, and a pool of blood spreading around his head.

I checked his pulse, but I was too late to save him.

Meatball growled and stalked toward the door of the old gallery.

My shaking grew worse. If this had only just happened, the killer could still be here, and I could be their next victim.

Meatball's growls grew deeper and more menacing.

I stepped away from Herbert, and mustering every ounce of courage I had, turned to face whoever was behind me.

"Holly!" Lady Philippa whispered as she appeared in the doorway.

"Oh my goodness! You gave me a scare. I thought you were the killer come back to finish me off." I hurried over to her. "I said to stay in your room. It's not safe down here."

"I couldn't leave you on your own." She looked past me and her eyes grew large. "Oh! It's that charming man who's been working on the restoration project."

"Yes, it's Herbert. Lady Philippa, go back to your room. Did you call Campbell?" I gently tugged on her elbow, but she refused to move.

"I called him. I told him what was going on. He wasn't happy to hear from me."

"What did you tell him?"

"That I'd had a vision about someone being killed by a statue of my relative."

I groaned. Campbell had no time for Lady Philippa's predictions. "Okay. So long as he's on his way. Now, you need to leave. What if—"

A scuffling in one corner of the old gallery made me freeze. I clutched Lady Philippa's elbow.

"What was that?" she whispered.

I swallowed, the shaking in my limbs returning.

Meatball was stalking toward the shadowy corner where the noise had come from.

"Come back, Meatball. Get away from there," I whispered.

There was more scuffling from the same corner.

I peered into the gloom. My eyes were getting used to the darkness, and I could make out a human-looking shadow exactly where Meatball was going.

"Lady Philippa, you need to move. Get up the stairs now."

"I'm not going anywhere," she said. "We've got them trapped. That's the killer. This is the only way out. We stand firm, and there's nothing they can do."

The shadow moved. A large, dark looming shape leaped over Meatball and charged at us.

Meatball growled and barked, chasing after the figure.

I stood in front of Lady Philippa to protect her as the killer barged into me, whacking me on the arm with something hard. Then they were gone, out the door.

Meatball gave chase.

I turned to Lady Philippa, holding my throbbing arm. "Are you okay?"

"I'm fine. Who was that? I didn't get a look at their face."

"Stay here. I need to stop them." I raced out after Meatball and across the gravel.

Meatball was still tracking the intruder, but they'd gotten a good head start, and Meatball only had little legs.

I gave chase, my arm still throbbing. It didn't feel broken, but whatever they'd hit me with had been hard and cold, and my pajamas weren't much protection. I limp-raced over the gravel and onto the lawn.

I couldn't see the intruder clearly. They were dressed in black and had their sweater hood pulled up and tied tight so only their eyes were visible.

They dodged into some trees.

Meatball launched himself after them.

I rushed after them, my breath gasping out of me and my ankle throbbing along with my arm. I slowed as I reached the trees and took several deep breaths, trying to calm my racing heart.

"Meatball," I whispered. "Where are you?"

I couldn't hear anyone moving around. Even the trees were quiet, as if they were waiting to see who would make the next move.

"I know you're in here. I've seen you. You won't get away with this. You need to give yourself up." I took a few steps and cocked my head, listening hard. "You're in enough trouble. Don't make this any worse by hiding."

A quiet bark had me racing ahead. Meatball must have found them.

I yelped as a blast of movement shot out in front of me, and the shadowy figure raced away.

Meatball was hot on the killer's heels. For a second, he grabbed their pant leg, but whoever it was, they kicked out.

I gasped, feeling sick as Meatball was struck.

He lost his hold and flipped onto his back. But he was immediately up and running again.

My heart was in my throat. "Don't you dare hurt my dog." I ignored my throbbing arm and painful ankle as I chased the killer. They weren't getting away. They'd just made this personal. No one kicked my dog.

I sped out of the trees. Whoever it was, they were heading back to the castle. Why would they do that? If they went inside, they'd be trapped.

A door slammed, and Meatball yipped a high-pitched bark suggesting he'd been hurt.

I was queasy with worry as I raced to the side door Meatball stood by.

He was licking one paw and whining.

"Are you okay?" I carefully ran my hands over him.

He raised his paw and whimpered.

I scooped him up and snuggled him against me. "Let's get you to the vet." I tried the door, but the handle refused to turn. The killer must have locked it from the inside.

I hurried around the outside of the castle and was just in time to spot a shadowy figure moving past one of the windows. I banged on the glass.

Whoever it was, they jumped, but kept on moving.

I whacked the glass again. "I'll find you and make you pay for what you've done to Meatball. And Herbert." I kissed the top of Meatball's head. Even though Herbert was dead, my prime concern was Meatball.

"Holly," Lady Philippa called out.

I was already heading back to the east turret, my phone in my hand as I found a number for an emergency vet.

"I'm right here, Lady Philippa."

"Did the killer get away?" She appeared in the entrance.

"They did. I think they're inside the castle, though. Where's Campbell?"

"He's dealing with Herbert. And he's called the police." She hurried over. "What's happened to Meatball?"

"I'm not sure. He hurt his paw when he was chasing the killer. Give me a minute, Lady Philippa." I made a call to the emergency vet, but it went straight to voicemail. I kissed Meatball's head again. I had to get him looked at. I tried the number one more time, with no luck.

I swiped my hand across my cheek. Why weren't they answering?

"I know someone who can help Meatball," Lady Philippa said. "He's semi-retired, but he looks after the sheep and goats that graze our lower fields. He'll come out. He's not far from here. Give me your phone. No, I never know how to use those things. I'll find his number, and you call him. I'll speak to him."

"Thanks." I sniffed back tears as I gently examined Meatball's paw. It was puffy and bleeding. It looked like it had been squashed.

He whimpered and licked it.

"We'll get you sorted. Don't worry."

Campbell appeared in the doorway of the east turret, his shoulders tight. "What's going on? And what's the matter with Meatball?"

"He was chasing after the killer and got injured. Lady Philippa's finding a vet to come out and see him."

Campbell strode over. He ran his hands over Meatball, then examined the paw. "Poor little guy. It doesn't look broken, but he must be in a lot of pain."

Meatball licked Campbell's hand.

Lady Philippa raced out with a number on a piece of paper. "Here it is."

I dialed the number and then let her talk to the vet.

"So, what happened?" Campbell said. "I got a garbled message from Lady Philippa talking about visions and statues."

"Same here. She left several messages on my phone, but I'd fallen asleep, so I missed them. By the time I figured out what she was telling me, I was too late. I ran over here as quickly as I could and was arriving when I heard a fight in the old gallery. I discovered Herbert dead. The killer was hiding in the shadows."

"Why is Lady Philippa involved in this?" Campbell glanced over at Lady Philippa, who was still talking on the phone. "You know how fragile she is."

"That wasn't my choice. I told her to stay in her room, but she came down."

"It's all arranged." Lady Philippa walked back and handed me my phone. "The vet will be here in fifteen minutes."

"Thank you so much, Lady Philippa," I said.

"Anything for this lovely boy. Now, what are we going to do about the body in the old gallery?"

"Everything's being dealt with. Are you feeling up to answering a few questions?" Campbell said.

"Of course. Anything to help."

"Did you hear something in the old gallery that made you realize there was a problem?" Campbell said.

"No, I didn't hear anything," Lady Philippa said. "I already told you, I had a vision. And a new ghost appeared in my rooms. I believe it was the ghost of Bluebell Brewster."

Campbell cut a glare my way. "Someone came into your room and told you there was a fight downstairs?"

"I didn't know anything about the fight until the ghost told me. I came down to see what Holly was doing, and we almost saw the killer. I didn't see their face, though. It's most annoying."

Campbell exhaled a soft sigh. "Thanks. That'll be all for now. Holly, take Lady Philippa back to her rooms. This has been a stressful situation. It can't be doing her any good."

"Campbell Milligan, don't talk about me as if I'm not here. And you don't need to worry about me. This is the most excitement I've had in months." Lady Philippa drew herself upright. "I'm telling you, Bluebell Brewster warned me this was about to happen. It took me a while to understand her. New ghosts are often confused, and she kept disappearing and only talking in partial sentences. I phoned Holly as soon as I realized what Bluebell was telling me. But I'm not great at using my phone, so I wasn't sure if my messages got through. I also have that silly prediction text on, and it kept spelling out the wrong words."

"Predictive text," Campbell muttered.

"Oh! That makes sense. You kept saying gallop horses in your messages," I said.

She tutted. "I meant to say get help. Gallop horses. Whoever invented prediction text is a fool."

"The messages got through to me, but I'd fallen asleep. I got here as soon as I could," I said.

"I know. You did your best," Lady Philippa said.

"If I'd have arrived sooner, I could have seen the killer's face," I said.

"And probably been harmed yourself," Campbell said. "Lady Philippa, you must have had a bad dream."

"I often dream about my ghosts, but I was absolutely awake when this new one appeared. She had a sharp look about her. It'll take time to get her to fit in with everyone else."

A muscle flexed in Campbell's jaw. "There's no such thing as ghosts."

There was a cracking noise over our heads. A large white shape loomed out of the darkness.

Campbell leaped out of the way a second before a large urn smashed to the ground just where he'd been standing.

Lady Philippa shrieked, and I jumped back, clutching Meatball tightly to me.

I stared at the shattered urn. "Where did that come from?"

"We have them on the roof. It must have been the ghosts," Lady Philippa said. "They don't like it when people talk badly about them. Do you believe me now, Campbell?"

He looked down at the urn fragments, and then up at the roof. "Anything could have dislodged that."

"It's an enormous stone urn," I said. "Even you'd have trouble shoving that off the roof."

"No, I wouldn't. The work in the old gallery could have disturbed it." He licked his lips and glanced around.

"I know exactly what moved that urn. You need to be nicer to my ghosts, or they may follow you home and keep throwing things at you," Lady Philippa said.

"Holly, please. I have to focus on Herbert's murder. Take Lady Philippa to her rooms. Make sure she has everything she needs." Campbell glanced away. "Here come the police. I need to get them up to speed."

"We should get you inside," I said to Lady Philippa. "And I want to give Meatball a thorough check over before the vet gets here."

"Then you must come up with me. It's warm and safe in there. We'll take the best care of Meatball. Follow me." Lady Philippa hurried inside and up the stairs at a surprisingly quick pace, leaving me limping slowly behind her.

I was out of breath and my ankle was screaming at me by the time I'd reached the top. I stumbled my way along the corridor into Lady Philippa's rooms.

"Put Meatball on the bed." Lady Philippa laid a velvet pillow on her enormous double bed.

"Are you sure you don't mind? He'll be fine on the floor."

"Of course not. Horatio, make sure you're not mean to Meatball. He's been in the wars. He tried to stop a killer."

Lady Philippa's grumpy, overweight corgi grumbled and rolled onto his side. He opened one eye, looked at Meatball, and shut it again.

I placed Meatball down and gently stroked him. Other than his paw, he seemed fine.

"Would you like a biscuit?" Lady Philippa said to him.

"I'm sure he would, but maybe he shouldn't have anything to eat. The vet may need to give him some medication."

"Of course. He's such a brave boy." She stroked his head.

"Tell me more about this vision you had." I settled next to Meatball and made sure he was comfortable. "Did you really see Bluebell's ghost?"

"It had to be her. I'd seen her a few times when she was working downstairs, so I recognized her. I knew it would be risky to contact Campbell and tell him about my ghost. That's why I called you."

I looked around for any signs of Bluebell's ghost. "Did she tell you who wanted Herbert dead?"

"No, nothing so helpful. I didn't understand what she wanted. She kept gesturing to the stairs and only saying fragments of sentences. It always happens with the new ones. I'll get a more established ghost to take her under their wing and show her how things work. That's if she decides to stay around. They don't always. But those who've had traumatic deaths often struggle to move on."

I glanced around her room, which was warm and cozy. I couldn't imagine a less likely place to find a group of ghosts hanging out. "Did she tell you anything that could be useful?"

Lady Philippa closed her eyes for a few seconds. "She said something had been stolen."

"What sort of thing?"

"I'm not sure. But I have a feeling these murders have to do with greed. Someone is taking things that don't belong to them. They'll do anything to stop from being discovered."

There was a knock at the door. Lady Philippa hurried over and opened it. "Come in, Cedric. Our patient's in here."

An elderly man with an impressive white beard walked in. He had on a gray overcoat over a pair of red flannel pajamas.

He gave me a kind smile. "I came as quickly as I could. Where's the patient?"

"He's here," I said. "This is Meatball. I think he got his paw caught in a door."

"Hello there." Cedric set down his bag and let Meatball sniff his fingers. "Will you be a good boy and let me examine you?"

"He doesn't bite," I said. "But he's not that friendly with vets."

Cedric chuckled softly, his eyes full of warmth. "Most animals aren't. They know we're going to poke them around and probably stick a thermometer somewhere sensitive. We'll take it slow and see what we find."

Horatio grumbled. He rolled off the bed and slunk under it.

Meatball whimpered as Cedric examined his sore paw.

"I don't think it's broken," I said, keeping a reassuring hand on Meatball's back.

"No, but it is badly bruised, and a claw has been torn off. He's lucky not to have worse damage." Cedric spent a couple of minutes checking over Meatball.

"How bad is it?" I said.

"Overall, he's in excellent health. I'll give him pain relief and clean the foot. My concern is he may continue to lick it. That'll slow the healing. I'll give you a cone to put around his head."

"Meatball will hate that," I said.

"He may need to wear it for a few days, just in case." Cedric petted Meatball. "Let's get to work and get you fixed up. Then I'm sure Lady Philippa will have a treat for you."

"Of course. He'll enjoy all the biscuits he likes once he's been through this. He's our hero dog," she said.

There was a tap on the door. Campbell appeared. "How's Meatball?"

"He'll be fine," I said. "Nothing's broken."

"Good. Have you got a minute? We need to talk."

Chapter 17

I left Meatball with Cedric, my pulse returning to normal now I knew there was nothing seriously wrong with his paw, and headed into the corridor with Campbell.

"How's everything going with Herbert?" I asked.

"We've secured the scene," Campbell said.

"And the killer? Whoever it was, they went back inside the castle."

"My men are searching the castle and grounds. So far, nothing has shown up. Are you sure they went inside?"

"Yes!"

"We'll keep looking. Has Lady Philippa made any more sense?"

"She always makes sense."

Campbell simply raised his eyebrows.

"Okay, so she sometimes mentions ghosts, but it's an eccentricity. You don't have to be so mean about her. She's sensitive to certain things. Maybe she picked up a vibration—"

"I'm not interested in hearing about weird vibrations. I'm interested in what I can actually see. Tell me what you saw when you confronted the killer in the old gallery."

I glanced back at the door where I could hear the gentle voice of Cedric still talking to Meatball. "It happened in a rush. I didn't get a good look at the killer. I got there just after Herbert had been killed. Lady Philippa came down from her rooms. I was looking around when Meatball sensed someone. He was walking toward them when they ran at us. I got whacked on the arm, then they raced off."

"Did you get injured?"

I rubbed my tender arm. "There'll be a bruise, but I'm okay."

"Give me a description of the attacker."

"I really didn't see much. I was in shock after finding Herbert and then being hit. They were dressed in black and had a sweatshirt with a hood on. It was pulled across their face, so I could barely see them. Meatball chased them, and I followed. I made sure Lady Philippa stayed here and called you."

"You shouldn't have chased the killer. You should have been protecting Lady Philippa."

I arched an eyebrow. "Isn't that your job?"

"I didn't know she was in trouble."

"Neither did I until Lady Philippa called me. And you know why that was. You never believe a word she says."

"You're telling me you believe in her premonitions, being able to dream about people dying, and ghosts?"

I glared up at him. "Maybe I do. How do you explain the urn that almost squashed you?"

"Gravity."

"It's a big coincidence, though. You were complaining about the ghost theory and then you're almost killed by an invisible assailant."

"Holly, this castle is ancient. Stone crumbles, cement loosens, and things fall."

I crossed my arms over my chest. "I'm not saying I believe in ghosts, but you should give Lady Philippa more credit."

He was quiet for a few seconds. "She was left in a vulnerable position."

"But I had an opportunity to catch the killer. I could have solved this mystery."

He shook his head. "This is my fault she was put at risk. I'll suggest to the family that I post a member of my team in the east turret full-time."

"Lady Philippa will hate that. Alice and Rupert are always talking about locking her up. If you put a guard outside her room, she really will feel like a prisoner."

"It's for her own good. She may have been the one whacked over the head if she'd confronted the killer."

I hated the thought of Lady Philippa at risk, but she was sturdier than they thought she was.

"So, this killer. Do you think they're bumping off members of the restoration team? First Bluebell, and now Herbert," I said.

"It looks like it."

"Why do that? Is there something in this painting they're restoring the killer doesn't want anyone else to see?"

"This can't be about the painting. It's hundreds of years old. It won't show anything incriminating. This has something to do with the team working on it."

"Whoever it is, they must be getting desperate, because they almost got caught this time."

"Maybe this murder wasn't planned," Campbell said. "Herbert could have figured out something was wrong and put himself in danger. Which was exactly what Lady Philippa did when she contacted you instead of me."

I was overtaken by a huge yawn and quickly covered my mouth with my hand. "I'm too freaked out to think straight."

"More like, you're too tired. You do realize, you're still wearing your pajamas?"

"These are comfy. And I had no time to get changed."

He smirked. "You should go home. I've got things covered. The police will be a while looking at Herbert's body and checking the scene."

"The rest of the family need to know what's going on. There's a killer running around inside their castle."

"I'm not so sure there is. Are you certain it was the same person?" Campbell said. "My men have reported in nothing."

I took a minute to get my thoughts in order. "I ... well, it was a figure dressed in black, just like the one I'd been chasing. And I heard a door slam. I assumed they'd gone inside."

"You didn't see them go through the door?" Campbell said.

"No, but Meatball was ahead of me. He was chasing them. That's when he got his paw injured. The killer must have slammed the door to stop Meatball getting in."

"We have cameras inside the castle. If they did sneak inside, we'll see them."

"You don't have cameras everywhere. And if this killer is familiar with the castle's layout, they'd be able to avoid being spotted. It's dark inside, and they're dressed in black. They could hide in the shadows and sneak past the cameras."

He sighed. "We'll keep looking. And I have men outside the bedrooms, so the family won't come to any harm. Make sure you lock your own door when you get back to your apartment."

"I'll get Gran to stand guard with a pineapple."

"A pineapple?"

I waved my hand in the air. "Don't worry about it." I took a step and stumbled as my ankle protested. I almost fell, just managing to grab hold of Campbell's arm to stop from tumbling to the floor.

"You're impossible. You've messed up your ankle again." He shook his head. "When will you learn to look after yourself?"

"When I don't have to chase after a killer and help my injured dog," I said.

"Sit down on the window ledge," Campbell said.

"I don't need to. It'll be okay once I get going." I tried my ankle again and frowned. Maybe it wouldn't.

"Holly, sit. Now. I have something that'll help."

"What is it?"

He pointed at the wide, low stone window ledge.

I held onto his arm as I limped my way over and sank down with a pained sigh.

Campbell knelt in front of me and shoved up the leg of my pajamas.

I pulled my leg away. "What are you doing?"

"It's an old army trick. Do you want your ankle to feel better, or not?"

"You're not going to chop my foot off, are you?"

He smirked. "If I did, you'd still find a way to interfere in every investigation I run."

"Which doesn't happen anymore, since we work together."

"You seem to be doing a lot of working alone on this one."

"Not out of choice. I'd have preferred it if you'd been chasing the killer tonight. Then my ankle wouldn't have flared up, and Meatball's paw wouldn't have been injured."

"Give me your foot," he said.

I inched my leg out.

He grabbed hold of it and balanced it on his knee. Then he clapped his hands together and rubbed them briskly.

"This is a technique taught to me by an old commander. If you generate enough heat between your hands and apply it to an injury, it brings down the inflammation. It's temporary, but provides instant relief. It's good when you're in a tight spot and have no option but to run."

I gasped as he wrapped his hot hands around my ankle. Instantly, the throbbing eased. "That feels amazing."

"Remember, it's not healing anything. If you overuse this ankle, the pain will get worse. You have to rest. Everyone is telling you to do so. You never listen to anyone's advice."

"I really am trying. Sometimes, you have to put other people's needs before your own. What do they say in the military? Who dares wins? Fortune favors the brave?"

Campbell rolled his eyes. "There's a French military unit who have the motto the dead get up. They don't. You don't need to learn that the hard way. All you should focus on is making me more delicious cake. It's much better for you than trying to figure out these murders."

"I could create a motto for cake makers. Making life sweeter with every bite. All you need is cookies. Baking people happy. Keep calm and eat cake. Cake makes—"

Campbell squeezed my ankle. "Stop talking, Holmes."

Rupert rushed through the door and along the corridor, slowing when he saw us. His gaze went to Campbell's hands wrapped around my ankle. "Am I interrupting?"

Campbell placed my foot on the floor and stood. "No, Lord Rupert. I was just looking after Holly's ankle."

Rupert blinked several times, then laughed. "For a second, it looked like you were about to propose to her."

I roared out a laugh. "That'll never happen."

Rupert walked closer, a cautious look in his eyes. "I heard a noise in the castle. I came out of my room to see what was going on and found a guard outside. Is it true about Herbert?"

"It is," I said. "We almost caught the killer, but they got away."

"And now Holly needs to go home," Campbell said.

"I'll see if I can remember anything else about the killer," I said to him. "Tonight's been a bit of a blur, though."

"You need to get to bed. Rest your foot," Campbell said.

"I'll take you home." Rupert hurried to my side.

"That's sweet of you, but you should check on your granny. She might be in shock. She was right there with me. The killer barged past us."

"Oh! Yes, then I should check in on her. She's got a weak heart. Are you sure I can't do anything to help you, though?" Rupert said.

"You could bring Meatball down for me," I said.

"Of course. Where's Meatball?"

"With your gran and the vet. He's also been injured. The vet's with him now. Lady Philippa's been great at getting help for him. They should be done, but I don't want him walking down all those steps on a sore paw."

"I'll make sure he's safe," Rupert said. "How are you going to get home?"

Campbell sighed. "I'll take her. I'll get the SUV and drive Holly to her door."

"That's an excellent idea," Rupert said. "I'll go and see how things are with Granny and Meatball." He hurried away along the corridor.

"Now you've got Lord Rupert running around after you," Campbell said. "You need to make sure your influence doesn't go to your head."

"He doesn't run around after me. Friends help each other out."

"Sure. Friends. I'll go get the car."

I remained where I was, gently twisting my ankle. Campbell was a miracle worker. Although it still ached, my ankle felt much less painful. I'd have to learn that trick.

A few minutes later, Rupert appeared in the doorway with a small bag. Meatball was in his arms, wagging his tail and trying to lick Rupert's cheek. Cedric was right behind him.

"How's Meatball doing?" I said.

"All good," Cedric said. "The paw is badly swollen and there's some damage to the nails, and one of the pads has a deep cut on it. Everything's been cleaned and checked over. I haven't put him in a head cone, but I'll leave one for you in case he worries the injury. I also provided you with some socks. He needs to rest his paw as much as possible, so no long walks. Short trips out to use the toilet and get some air, but that's it for five days. When he goes outside, he must wear socks on his injured paw, or it'll get infected."

"Whatever you say. I just want him to get better."

"He'll be fine. I've given him some antibiotics, and I'll leave you with some pills for pain relief and a short course of oral antibiotics. He'll need one a day for seven days. He's a strong lad and healthy as an ox. He'll get through this. His paw will be fine."

"Thanks so much," I said. "What do I owe you?"

Cedric waved a hand. "It's all sorted. Lady Philippa has dealt with everything. Any problems, give me a call. I'll check up on him once he's finished his antibiotics. I've given Lord Rupert the pills, cone, and socks for Meatball. Take care, both of you." He petted Meatball on the head, then strolled off down the stairs.

I fussed over Meatball for a minute, and he wagged his tail. "I'm so glad he's okay. I don't know what I'd do without him."

"Cedric used to look after the Queen's horses," Rupert said. "He's the best in the business. He mainly deals with equine animals, but he knows everything. Meatball is in safe hands when it comes to his recovery."

Campbell marched up the stairs. "The car's outside."

I held onto Rupert's shoulder and limped slowly down the stairs, one painful step at a time.

He put Meatball on the back seat of the SUV, and I eased myself onto the seat next to him.

"Take care, Holly. I'll come and see how you're doing tomorrow," Rupert said.

We said our goodbyes, and Campbell drove us away.

"What happens next with Herbert's murder?" I said.

"Don't worry about that. I'll get it sorted."

"Don't shut me out."

"I'm not. But you need to rest. We can talk about it tomorrow."

I sank back into the seat and gave another yawn. I really was exhausted. Chasing after a killer had taken it out of me.

It seemed to have done the same for Meatball. His eyes were already closed, and he was gently snoring.

We arrived at my apartment, and Campbell helped me out. He lifted Meatball off the seat, along with his bag of goodies, and carried him to the door, while I limped beside him.

Gran yanked open the door. "Holly! What have you been up to? I woke when I heard the front door go."

"Holly's hurt her ankle again. Meatball's hurt his paw. You need to look after them." Campbell thrust Meatball into Gran's arms.

"You've both been injured?" Gran narrowed her eyes. "Campbell, did you have anything to do with this?"

"Gran! None of this is Campbell's fault. Let's get inside."

"Holly needs to go to bed," Campbell said. "There's been another murder. Keep your doors and windows locked." He turned and strode back to the SUV.

Gran stared at me. "Another murder?"

"Make me some hot chocolate, and I'll tell you everything."

Chapter 18

I rolled over and stretched. Meatball was lying alongside me in bed, snoring softly.

I gently tickled his belly. "How's your paw doing?"

His eyes opened, and he thumped his tail against the pillow.

I did a careful exploration of his injured paw. Although he whimpered a little, he let me look.

"It seems to be healing. I need to find something tasty to hide your pill in, to make sure you keep getting better."

I tested my ankle, twisting it carefully from side to side. It felt tender, but not too bad.

I wasn't sure I'd sleep the previous night, what with everything that had gone on, but I'd passed out alongside Meatball after filling Gran in about everything that had happened at the castle.

I took a shower, got dressed, and headed down to the kitchen.

There were fresh muffins on the table and a note from Gran.

Sorry, had an appointment I couldn't cancel this morning. Hope the ankle is okay. Enjoy the muffins. Love Gran.

I made Meatball his breakfast, hid his pill in a piece of sausage, and then ate a muffin. I wanted to get to the castle early to find out what was happening about Herbert.

A frown crossed my face as I looked down at Meatball. There was no way he'd be able to handle a walk to the castle. I'd need to take it easy, too. We needed something to help us.

I opened the closet where Gran kept her shopping trolley, pulled it out, and undid it. It was large, with a roomy interior. It could be just what I needed.

"What do you reckon, Meatball? Would you be happy in here?"

He trotted over and had a good sniff of the trolley.

"If I angle it right, you can lay on your belly and still see out the top. Shall we give it a go? I don't want to leave you here on your own. You may get in trouble with your paw. And I don't want to force you to wear a collar of shame."

He was happy enough for me to pick him up and place him in the trolley. He scrambled around a bit, but when I added a couple of toys and a favorite chew stick, he soon settled down.

I nodded. "Let's do this." I eased my sore foot into a sensible pair of flat shoes, tugged on my jacket, and headed out of the apartment with Meatball in the trolley.

It was slow going, but it worked. Meatball seemed to enjoy his new mode of transport, and after a quick pit stop so he could get out and do his toilet, he clambered back in and we headed to the castle.

I slowed as I got near the main gate. Rupert was standing outside, talking to Sara.

He stood very close to her, his head bent as she talked to him.

Sara placed a hand on Rupert's chest and laughed.

I frowned, my stomach clenching. What did Rupert think he was doing?

I watched them for several minutes. They were flirting! Did Rupert like Sara?

The idea didn't sit well with me. We weren't dating, and I had no claim over him, but I hated the thought of him being with anyone else. I couldn't have him, but I didn't want anyone else to have him.

These thoughts were definitely not those of a rational woman. All this murder business was getting to me.

Sara eventually walked away. I hurried over as best I could, using the trolley to help me keep some weight off my ankle. "Rupert! I'm surprised to see you about so early. Did you have a breakfast date with Sara?"

"Holly! I've been thinking about you all night. How are you?" He glanced at the trolley and smiled. "I see you've got things fixed up for Meatball."

"We're fine. What were you doing with Sara?"

Rupert glanced over his shoulder in the direction Sara had gone. "Oh, just chatting. She seems like an agreeable woman. Very friendly."

"Friendly? Yes, she is. I didn't realize you two knew each other so well."

"We don't. Not really. I've been by the restoration project numerous times, though. Sara's always there and she's easy to chat to."

"You sound fond of her."

His eyes widened a fraction. "Would that be a problem if I was?"

I sucked in a breath. "No, you can date who you like. Why should I care?"

"Oh! Well, perhaps I will. I may even ask Sara out."

I set the trolley upright and glowered at him. "Sara's dating Justin. Are you happy to mess with their relationship just because you're fond of her?"

"Ah, no. I didn't know about that. Sara never mentioned it. Of course, I haven't asked if she was single. You ... you just put the idea in my head. I don't really know why I said it. It was silly of me."

I shrugged, trying desperately to look like I didn't care. "It's a good idea. You should date. Maybe pick someone who's single, though." I wasn't being rational, I knew that. Rupert deserved to be happy. He needed to find someone, and his parents had plans for him to do just that. But it didn't fill me with joy to know he'd eventually find a woman he wanted to marry. And it wouldn't be me.

Rupert rocked back on his heels. He cleared his throat several times. "Holly, I'd like a private audience with you."

I took a step back and bumped into the trolley. "Why? Are you going to fire me? You can date who you like. It's none of my business."

"No! It's not that." He ran a hand through his messy blond hair. "This has nothing to do with your job. I need to speak to you on your own."

"Holly!" Campbell strode around the side of the castle and headed toward us.

Rupert sighed. "I suppose he wants to talk to you about murder. Unless he's going to rub your ankle again."

"That was nothing. He was helping me."

Rupert hummed under his breath. "I suppose so. But he was being very familiar with you."

"He was only touching my ankle. This is the twenty-first century. I'm allowed to let a man do that. It doesn't mean he has to marry me."

"No! Of course not. I just … I didn't like it."

He sounded jealous. I didn't know what to say. I let out a breath I didn't realize I'd been holding. Things suddenly felt tense between me and Rupert.

He touched my elbow. "Holly, will you meet with me?"

"I can meet you after work today. I should be done by six o'clock. Can you give me a hint of what you want to talk about?"

"No. In two days' time."

"Why then?"

Rupert backed away. "Everything will be sorted by then. I hope."

"Sorted? I don't understand. What needs sorting before we can meet up?"

Campbell stopped beside me. He glanced at Rupert. "Is everything okay, Lord Rupert?"

"Everything is great." Rupert turned and dashed away.

I stared after him. "He was being really weird. Do you know what's wrong with him?"

"I don't question my employer about any unusual behavior they choose to exhibit. I thought you'd want to hear about the murder."

I shook my head, my attention still on Rupert.

"Is that a no, you don't want to hear about Herbert's murder?"

I turned to Campbell. "Oh, no. I do. I mean, are you sure there isn't a problem with Rupert?"

Campbell bent and petted Meatball's head. "Not that I know of. How's this furry guy doing?"

"He had a good night. We both did. And he took his pill this morning. So, Herbert's murder?"

Campbell nodded. "Here are the basics. He was definitely killed. There are no prints on the statue used to strike the back of his head. And there's no sign of the killer entering the castle after Herbert was murdered."

"Are you sure?"

"My team doesn't make mistakes. The security footage has been viewed and all rooms checked. No one is hiding in the castle. You must have seen someone else sneaking around."

I was sure I hadn't, but I had no way to prove it. "There's nothing at the crime scene to help us figure this out?"

"Nothing useful."

"What about the urn that was shoved off the top of the castle?"

"What about it?"

"Could the killer have done it to cause a distraction? It would have given them time to get away."

"I had a couple of guys look around the site. There was nothing to suggest anyone had been up there."

"Which supports Lady Philippa's ghost theory," I said.

"It also supports my crumbling cement and gravity theory. We've found nothing so far that leads us to who killed Herbert."

Meatball barked and tried to jump out of the trolley.

Campbell scooped him up and placed his front paws over his shoulder, while cupping his butt in his arm.

Meatball seemed happy to stay there, so I walked slowly alongside Campbell toward the kitchen, pulling the trolley behind me.

"I was hoping I'd get a flash of inspiration last night about the killer," I said. "I didn't remember anything useful, though."

"We've also drawn a blank."

"Should we be looking for one killer or two?" I said.

"Everything pointed at Herbert as Bluebell's killer," Campbell said. "I didn't get to speak to him before he was killed, though. I could have gotten a confession and have had at least one of these murders solved."

"I wouldn't mind taking another look in the old gallery," I said.

"There's nothing to see. The place has been swept for evidence. And I'm not letting the conservation crew in today. What are you hoping to find?"

"I'm not sure. Something that could jog my memory? Give us a clue as to who killed Herbert, and possibly

Bluebell."

Campbell shrugged. "Why not? I'm getting desperate. Let's go take a look now."

We headed into the old gallery. I stopped by the entrance and looked at the spot where I'd discovered Herbert dead on the floor. I shuddered and looked away.

"You doing okay, Holmes?"

"I'm not going to faint if that's what you're worried about." I limped forward. "The killer was over in that left corner. He must have been hiding by the pile of equipment, trying to conceal himself. It's only when my eyes adjusted to the gloom that I saw him."

"You definitely think it was a him?"

"There's a fifty-fifty chance I'm right," I said. "If it was a guy, he wasn't tall. But he charged at me so quickly, I didn't get a good look." I poked around for several minutes before returning to Campbell and Meatball. "Don't laugh at what I'm about to say."

"I'll do my best not to."

"Lady Philippa has information to suggest the killings are linked to a theft."

"Where's she getting her information from?" Campbell said.

"This is the bit you're not allowed to laugh at." I narrowed my eyes at him. "The ghosts told her."

Campbell closed his eyes for a second. "The ghosts?"

"They said these murders had to do with greed. We find out what's been stolen, and we could find our killer."

Campbell sighed. "Didn't we go over this ghost nonsense last night?"

"We did. But you've got to admit, Lady Philippa has a knack for predicting these things. And once or twice, when I've been in her rooms, I have felt cold spots and heard voices that I can't explain."

"That's called having an overactive imagination. You know Lady Philippa has funny turns. They make her see things."

"They aren't funny turns. They're …" I wasn't sure what they were. Maybe she was a genuine fortune teller.

"Go on, say it. She's making predictions about the future. Which isn't possible. Neither are ghosts."

There was a loud thud against one wall.

I stared at Campbell. "You're telling me that wasn't a ghost letting you know how unhappy she is about being dismissed."

"Take hold of Meatball. I'll prove to you it wasn't a ghost."

I caught hold of Meatball, and Campbell strode to a wood-paneled wall. He thumped one of the small panels, and a door appeared.

Alice tumbled out of it.

I gasped and then laughed. "What are you doing in there?"

Campbell caught hold of her to keep her on her feet. "Princess Alice. Is everything okay?"

"Oh! Of course. I … I was taking a stroll." Her cheeks burned bright pink as she clung to Campbell a little tighter than necessary.

"Inside the priest passages?" Campbell said.

She lifted her chin. "I can go anywhere I like inside the castle."

"Of course you can," Campbell said. He dropped his hold on her and stepped back.

Alice glanced at me but didn't meet my gaze for more than half a second.

"I've been trying to see you. It sounds like you've been busy," I said.

She backed into the priest passage. "I can't stop. Campbell, close the door on me."

"Alice, wait. I want to talk to you." I limped closer.

"Campbell, that's an order. Close the door, immediately."

He glanced at me and shut the door in Alice's face.

I stared at the wall. "Why doesn't she want to talk to me anymore?"

"I can't answer that," Campbell said.

I shook my head. "This whole family is weird. I'm glad I only work for them."

"Maybe not for much longer, if Lord Rupert has anything to do with it."

My jaw dropped. "Do you think he's going to fire me? I know I spoke out of turn. He can date whoever he likes. But he can't sack me for that comment. If he wants to date Sara, he can. But she's involved with Justin. I …" My words trailed off when I saw the confusion on Campbell's face.

"What are you talking about?"

"When you arrived this morning, Rupert was flirting with Sara. He said he was going to ask her out. I … I may have overstepped the mark by telling him it was a bad idea."

"You, overstepping the mark with members of the Audley family. I can't believe such a thing is possible."

"Your sarcasm isn't helping. But he said he wanted to see me. He wants a private audience. Why would he do that? It must be because he's giving me bad news. I can't lose this job. I love it here. I'll apologize. I'll promise not to interfere in his private life ever again."

Campbell shook his head. "Holly, for someone so smart, you can be dense at times. Go to work. I've got two murders to solve."

"What am I being dense about?"

Campbell strode away, leaving me with Meatball in the old gallery.

I kissed the top of Meatball's head, glanced around, and then limped back to the shopping trolley and placed him in it.

I'd seriously missed the point here, but I had no idea what was going on with Alice or Rupert. And I didn't like not knowing. Especially when it involved my future.

Chapter 19

I spent the rest of the morning in the kitchen, and was about to take my lunch break, when I spotted Sara, Greta, and Solomon striding around the gardens. Although I couldn't hear what they were saying, none of them looked happy.

"I'll take some lunch out to the restoration group," I said to Chef Heston.

"Why bother? They're not working today," he said.

"They still need to eat. I won't be long. They're just heading to the rose garden." I arranged a platter of sandwiches and lemon drizzle cake, then headed outside, keeping my pace steady to avoid aggravating my ankle.

Sara turned as I approached. Her expression was tight and her hands clenched. "Hey, Holly."

"Hi. I thought you could do with something to eat."

Greta turned and scowled at me. "We don't have time for lunch. We're working."

"I'll take a sandwich." Solomon investigated the platter I held out and selected cheese and tomato.

"I'm so sorry to hear about what happened to Herbert," I said.

Sara nodded, a glum expression on her face. "It's horrible news. I can't believe he's gone."

"Weren't you the one to discover him?" Greta's eyes narrowed.

"That's right," I said.

"What were you doing poking around our project so late at night?" Greta said. "In fact, you've constantly been getting under my feet. The police should question you. Have you been sabotaging this project?"

"Holly wouldn't do that," Sara said. "She's been great to us since we've been here. She always makes sure we get fed. Justin loves her because of all the delicious food she brings us."

"Thanks, Sara," I said. "I was there because I got a call from Lady Philippa. She lives alone above the old gallery. She was worried that something was going on, so I headed over to see her."

"This is the oddest place I've ever worked," Greta said. "Kitchen staff working so closely with the family."

"It may be odd, but the work is almost done," Sara said. "Another month of funding, and—"

"That's out of the question." Solomon took another sandwich, not sparing me a glance. "One murder we could handle, but two makes us look careless."

"We can't leave the painting partially restored," Sara said. "As I was just saying—"

"You've got until the end of the week," Solomon said. "But that's all the funding you're getting from Viking Investments."

"It does seem a shame to end things. The room will be stunning when it's done, and your clients will love it. Is there nothing I can do to persuade you to keep funding the project? I'll work my PR magic and fix things. Bluebell and Herbert will be forgotten in no time." Greta stroked her hand up Solomon's arm.

Sara gave a huff and turned away to stare at the roses.

I shared her anger. Greta talked about Herbert and Bluebell as if they were disposable and not worth remembering. Everyone deserved to be remembered.

Solomon smirked at Greta. "Even you're not that good. And this decision is out of my hands. The Board of Trustees voted first thing this morning. They can't be associated with a project where two people were killed. No matter how amazing the place will look, it isn't for us."

"We could say they were accidents," Greta said. "And now Herbert's dead, we don't need to worry about what happened to Bluebell."

"You think Herbert killed Bluebell?" I said.

Greta shot me an icy glare. "Who else would have done it? I had that security guy hassling me about Herbert's whereabouts the day after Bluebell died. I knew what he was thinking. Herbert was the killer. Now he's dead, that problem is solved."

"Even if he killed Bluebell, who killed Herbert?" I said.

They were silent for a moment. Sara chewed on a fingernail, Greta stared at her phone, and Solomon ate a sandwich.

"When I was questioned, I was told that someone was seen running away from Herbert's murder scene," Sara said. "Since you were there, did you get a look at them?"

"No. It was dark, and whoever it was surprised me. I did chase after them, but they got away. And they injured Meatball," I said.

Sara gasped. "Poor guy. He's such a sweetheart. How's he doing?"

"He won't be going on any long walks for a while, but he'll recover."

"Some people are monsters," Sara said.

"It wouldn't have made a difference if you'd caught the killer," Solomon said. "Viking Investments is done with this project. We don't want our investors getting twitchy because we're funding the wrong community project."

Sara glowered at Solomon. "You're lying. Viking Investments was already unhappy with this project because it was costing more than planned. Your trustees are just being tight fisted. You could easily fund the rest of the project."

"That's enough, Sara," Greta said. "Solomon's made his decision, and we have to respect that."

"Thank you, Greta. I appreciate your support. Although I didn't appreciate being dragged back here in the early hours of the morning to sort out this mess," he said.

"I feel your pain. I didn't welcome being woken by Sara pounding on my door, telling me what had happened to Herbert," Greta said.

"I could hardly go back to sleep," Sara said. "A man died!"

"How did you find out what happened to Herbert?" I said to Sara.

"I got up to use the bathroom. I glanced out the window and saw the east turret lit up and the cars outside. I woke Justin, and we went out to take a look. We didn't get very far. The police had the old gallery cordoned off. They told us there'd been an incident and someone died." Sara shook her head. "I still can't believe it. Herbert was such a decent man. He had a wobble over Bluebell, but we all understood that. Who would want him dead?"

"It's not important," Greta said. "Once you can get back on site, all you need to worry about is clearing away the equipment. This project is over."

"I expect Herbert thinks his murder is important to solve," I said.

Greta waved a hand in the air. "He can't think. He's dead. And it isn't our problem. I'm focused on damage control for the project and our funders."

Sara muttered under her breath and grabbed a sandwich from the tray.

"Did Herbert mention any concerns about his safety to any of you?" I asked.

"The man barely knew which day of the week it was, he was so caught up in his work. He never focused on anything else. And that included the reports I needed him to write," Greta said. "I suppose I'll have to sort those out, too."

"I'm sure we can massage the final paperwork requirements, since we're withdrawing our support." Solomon's smile turned leery as his gaze ran over Greta. "We'll figure something out. Let's schedule a one-on-one meeting."

I grimaced and looked away. Greta had no heart. All she cared about was saving face and making sure the paperwork was filed. And Solomon just wanted an excuse to get her into bed again.

"Maybe now this project is over, you'll get to spend more time with your fiancée," I said to Solomon.

His smug expression slipped, and he scowled at me. "I need to leave. I'm done with this place. You must be mad to live here."

I scowled at Solomon as he walked away. Greta hurried along beside him.

Sara shook her head. "He's a massive jerk. I think he was born that way. That's one thing I won't miss about this project. Most of the investors are like him. And I get it, they have a business to run, but what we do is so important. Now, it's all gone." She looked back at the castle. "I've loved working here, even with the murders. I've never been in a place quite like this."

"As odd as it is, I love it too. It's my home." I turned and also looked at the castle. How much longer would it be my home? I still had no idea what Rupert had planned for me. I had a worrying feeling it involved my future at the castle.

Sara ate another sandwich. "I'll work as hard as I can to make sure the painting looks good before we leave. I reckon we've got two days of work, and the rest of the time will be spent dismantling the equipment. It's such a shame."

"Where's Justin? Will he be helping out with the clean-up?"

"Sure. But we can't get into the old gallery, so he's taking a look around some of the other castle rooms. He's into all the wall hangings and wood paneling. And he's not great with confrontation. When he saw Solomon arrive, he grabbed his things and dashed off."

"I'll see if he wants the rest of this food," I said. "It would be a shame for it to go to waste."

"Justin never turns down food. He'll be grateful for it." Sara sighed. "I may as well go back to our apartment. There's not much else for me to do until they open the old gallery." She waved goodbye and walked away.

I munched on a sandwich as I mulled over the conversations I'd just had. Sara and Justin were in bed together when Herbert was killed, Solomon wasn't here, and it sounded like Greta had been in bed, too. They were the only suspects left in these murder investigations, but I had no clue what their motives would be for wanting Herbert dead.

"Is that food going spare?" Campbell strolled out of the trees and over to me.

"Have you been hiding there this whole time?" I held out the tray.

"No. But I saw you pestering the remaining suspects and wanted to see what you found out." He grabbed a piece of lemon drizzle cake and took a bite.

"Nothing helpful. I did find out that the restoration project is over."

Campbell nodded. "Yes. They'll be cleared out by the end of the week."

"And I also learned they all have alibis for when Herbert was killed. Well, I guess you need to check them out, but they all reckon they were nowhere near the old gallery last night."

"I've already checked them out."

"When did you do that?"

"While you were asleep. Sara and Justin were together, Solomon was two hundred miles away, and Greta was in bed."

"She was alone?"

"She was, but I don't think she did it." Campbell gestured to the castle.

I turned and walked along beside him. "Why do you think Greta's innocent?"

"She was busy on her phone at the time of the murder."

"That doesn't prove anything. You can use your phone anywhere. She could have been in the old gallery talking to someone just before she killed Herbert."

Campbell grinned. "She wasn't talking to anyone. And the kind of messages she was sending, you wouldn't write just before you murdered someone."

"You've lost me. What messages was Greta sending?"

"She was … communicating with Solomon. And it wasn't about work."

"They were fixing a date?"

"Their relationship is based more on physical need. They were sexting. And there were a few smutty images to go along with the dirty talk."

My cheeks grew warm. "Oh! Yes, good point. You wouldn't be feeling frisky just before you hit some guy over the head with a statue."

"Not unless there was something wrong with you. The phone records check out. There were no gaps in their communication to give either of them an opportunity to kill Herbert."

"So we're looking for a new mystery killer?" I said.

"Or we've missed something."

"Or one of the existing suspects has been so sneaky that they've fooled both of us."

"That's not possible," Campbell said. "If anyone here committed these murders, I'd have discovered them by now."

I shook my head. "I can't figure out a motive for any of them to want Herbert dead."

"He was struggling after Bluebell was killed. He could have annoyed someone."

"We saw him yelling at Sara and Justin on one occasion. He didn't seem to be doing so well. But that's no reason for them to kill him."

"It seems we're back to square one. If Herbert killed Bluebell, then there's nothing we can do about that, and we have no suspects or evidence to show who murdered Herbert."

I glanced at him. "You sound like you're giving up."

"I'm not. But I need to go back to basics. I'll dig into everyone's backgrounds again."

"You're suggesting you did miss something after all?"

He shot a glare my way. "I never miss anything. But I was focused on finding a connection between Bluebell and Herbert. Something concrete to link him to her death."

"Is there anything I can do?"

"Not for now. Keep an eye on everyone. Make sure they don't go sneaking off. I've asked them all to remain at the castle until this is sorted."

"I bet Solomon loved that."

"I don't care. The guy's a creep."

"I'm not arguing with that." We continued our slow walk. "Did you see Justin in the castle? He's always in need of a good feed, so I was taking him this food."

Campbell grabbed two sandwiches. "The last time I saw him, he was in the main hallway. He was asking to get access to the private family rooms. I told him no."

"Meany. He only wants to look at the wall coverings. He won't do any harm."

"It's still a no. The family deserve their privacy."

"Then he deserves all of these sandwiches." I gestured at the ones Campbell had grabbed.

He hid them behind his back. "What sandwiches?"

I tutted. "You'll lose your six pack if you eat all those carbs."

He patted his flat stomach and grinned. "Impossible."

I moved the tray out of his grasp. "Let me know if you find anything useful."

"Same here."

I turned and hurried away.

"Take it slowly, Holmes," Campbell said. "I can see you're still limping."

I waved a hand at him. My ankle was tender, but I could walk on it.

I headed into the main hallway and walked around for a few minutes until I spotted Justin. He was leaning against a wall, his nose almost touching it as he examined the detailing.

"It's a fascinating place, isn't it?" I said.

He jumped and stumbled back. "I didn't know anyone else was around."

"Sorry. I didn't mean to startle you. I saw Sara outside, and she thought you might like these." I held out the platter of food.

Justin licked his lips and grabbed the tray. "Thanks. We're almost out of food in the apartment. I only had a banana for breakfast." He stuck a whole sandwich in his mouth and chewed.

"I've been meaning to catch up with you. I hope you don't mind, but I borrowed a book you left in the old gallery. It was all about the castle's myths and legends."

He swallowed the sandwich. "I wondered where that had gone."

"It made for great reading. Have you got anything else I can borrow?"

Justin tapped a pile of books that sat on a nearby table. "Sara's always moaning at me for getting new books. I spend most of my money on them." He set down the food and looked through the pile. "This one's a good read. It's not too dry or academic."

I took it and flicked through the pages. It was all about the history of the castle. "Thanks. I'll have to bring back your other book."

"I've got plenty to keep me going, but I'll need them both back before I leave."

"I heard about the project being canceled. It's a pity. It would have been amazing to see that painting fully restored."

"I'm gutted. Apart from the fact two people have been murdered, I've enjoyed my time here. It must be great to live in a place like this. You're lucky."

I forced a smile. "I've enjoyed working here."

He tilted his head. "You're leaving, too?"

"No. Well, I'm not sure. Everything seems up in the air."

"Tell me about it. But that's the nature of my work. You're only ever given funding for a few months at a time. I need to find a more secure job. One with better pay. I love what I do, but there's only so many noodles and leftovers you can scrounge."

"Anytime you want to scrounge cake, you know where the kitchen is. Thanks for the book. I'll make sure I get it back to you before you leave."

"Thanks for the sandwiches. These will keep me going."

We said our goodbyes, and I headed back to the kitchen.

As I was flicking through the book, I spotted a section dedicated to the Audley Castle gold chalice. The chalice, sometimes called a goblet, had originated in the fourteenth century and been commissioned by King Edward the Third for his bride. When she displeased him by not giving him a child, he gifted it to the Audley family for their services to the Crown.

The chalice remained in the household until the late seventeen hundreds, when it was lost.

There were rumors it had reappeared over the years and was sometimes depicted in paintings or mentioned in texts. The last known sighting of the chalice was in the late eighteen hundreds, when it was detailed in an inventory of the castle. Since then, it had been missing.

That was a mystery I'd love to solve. No messy murder, no guilty parties, just a lump of gold in need of a home.

I pulled out my phone and messaged Alice. *What do you know about the missing Audley Castle chalice?*

The response was almost instant. *Not much. It's not real. If it is, it got lost ages ago. Why?*

I'm curious about it.

Don't be. I'm busy.

I frowned. *Doing what?*

I waited a moment, but no reply came back. I sighed and put away my phone. The mystery of the gold chalice would have to wait. I had cakes to bake and murder suspects to consider.

But I really wasn't sure which direction to turn when it came to Herbert's murder.

Chapter 20

The book Justin had given me was fascinating. I'd stayed up late last night, reading about the history of Audley Castle, and I kept returning to the section about the chalice. This intriguing, unique artifact seemed to be important to so many people.

I'd also run a search on the internet and found several groups, most of them involved in fantasy role-playing games, who had an interest in the chalice because of its perceived magical properties.

"How's your paw doing?" I looked down at Meatball. He was sitting beside me at the kitchen table as I ate breakfast the next morning.

He raised his sore paw, which was covered in a sock all ready for a short walk outside.

"How about we take a stroll to see Sara and Justin? I can return these books and ask them about the chalice. I bet they know more about it. They may even have more books I could borrow. Imagine if we found it."

We both finished our breakfasts, I made sure Meatball's protective sock was secure, then we took a gentle walk, doing a small circuit, before we came to the apartment Sara and Justin were in.

I walked along the gravel pathway and knocked at the door. There was no reply. I peered through the window, but the place looked empty.

I knocked again, then tried the handle. The door opened.

"Justin, it's Holly. I've brought back your books. Are you in here?" I stepped inside and looked into the kitchen. There were dirty dishes in the sink and discarded takeout cartons lying around. So much for surviving on just noodles.

I walked into the living room and wrinkled my nose. It looked like a teenage boy had been living in here. There were dirty mugs on the coffee table, clothes scattered around, a blanket and pillow crumpled on the end of the couch, and a musty smell in the air. It reminded me of school changing rooms.

"Justin needs to learn some homemaking skills," I muttered.

Meatball barked and trotted along the corridor.

"No, you don't. No investigating. This isn't our apartment."

He ignored me and pushed his way into the bedroom.

I set the books down on the coffee table and hurried after him. The chaos was even worse in this room. The bed hadn't been made, there was a wet towel on the floor, and several pairs of discarded socks.

"I don't know how Sara puts up with this. She must really like Justin to deal with all this mess."

There was a pile of books and papers beside the bed. I walked over and took a quick look. Most of the books were about Audley Castle. There was also a plan showing the castle's layout.

I kicked away a pair of red socks, knelt on the floor, and studied it. Several of the rooms had been crossed through with a red pen, and more had question marks over them. They were all the private family rooms.

I glanced at all the books about Audley Castle. Could Sara and Justin be looking for the mythical chalice? I didn't blame them. It was a fascinating puzzle.

There was a long list of phone numbers scribbled on a pad next to the building plan. All but one had been scratched through. Next to the remaining number was a huge 'yes' with exclamation points after it, and 'fifteen percent commission – rip off.'

I lifted the papers and rifled through them. There were printouts and pictures of the family's antique collections.

My stomach grumbled, and it wasn't because I was hungry. Sara and Justin wouldn't be stupid enough to steal from the castle, would they?

I pulled out my phone and dialed the number on the pad. It rang several times before being picked up.

"Columbia Auctioneers. This is Lawrence Falkirk speaking. How may I help you?"

My eyes widened. An auctioneer? Justin couldn't have anything to sell to them, and he certainly wasn't in the market for buying anything.

"Hello, is anybody there?"

"Yes. Sorry, I got distracted. Did you say you're an auctioneer?" I said.

"That's right. Are you interested in the upcoming auction in three weeks' time?"

"Um, yes. I could be. I … I had some information that items from Audley Castle would be coming up for auction. Are you the auctioneers selling them?"

"You mean the Audley gold coins?"

I sucked in a deep breath. "The coins? Yes, that's right. You have coins from the Audley family?"

There was a short pause. "May I ask how you found out about these particular items?"

"I have a personal interest. Someone mentioned the items would be coming up for auction. I'm interested in purchasing them, but I don't want to waste my time. What can you tell me about them?"

Lawrence sighed. "It's not going to be a secret for much longer. News like this is bound to slip out. I can't give you any specifics, because we're waiting for the coins to be verified. But I have seen them myself, and they look genuine."

"And if they are genuine?"

"They'll generate significant interest."

"How much do you think they'll go for?"

"I couldn't say. They're a rare acquisition. I'm anticipating six figures."

"Six figures!"

"Yes. Have you bought from us before? I'll have your name on our system, so I can alert you when the details become public."

"No, I've never bought from you. Where did you get them from?"

"I can't disclose that." Lawrence's tone grew cold. "We operate on a strict client confidentiality."

Meatball barked, and I looked up to see what had caught his attention. My eyes widened. Alice was standing in the doorway.

"I'm sorry, I didn't catch your name. Miss ..."

"Um ... um ... Alice Audley."

Alice tilted her head and looked at me.

"Could you repeat that? Is that Princess Alice Audley from Audley Castle?"

"Um ... yep. That's right. I've got to go." I ended the call and lowered the phone. "What are you doing here?"

"I was out for a walk when I saw you come in here. This isn't your apartment. What are you doing?"

I looked at the mess of papers, plans, and scribblings I'd discovered. "I'm not sure."

"And why are you using my name and pretending to be me on the phone?"

"Sorry about that. I blanked. I was looking right at you when the auctioneer asked me who I was. I blurted it out without thinking."

Alice looked at the pile of papers by my feet. "Auctioneer?"

"Alice, something weird is going on here. I found all this information and some auctioneers contact details. I called them, and they said they have coins that belong to your family. Have your parents been selling off assets?"

She stepped back. "I don't know anything about that. I shouldn't be here."

"Can you help me find out? It's strange that Justin is phoning auctioneers, and there just happens to be Audley gold coins coming up for auction. Do you think he stole them?"

"No. I don't know. Nothing's been reported missing. I need to go. I don't want to say anything I shouldn't." Alice turned and hurried away.

"Please! I need your help. You need to find out if these coins are missing."

She'd already reached the front door by the time I got out of the bedroom. I couldn't run after her, I'd only hurt my ankle.

"The coins aren't important," she said over her shoulder.

"They sound like they're worth a lot of money. Don't you care about them?"

"No. I've got much more important things on my mind."

"Tell me what they are. I could be able to help. Why do you keep avoiding me? What have I done wrong?"

Alice stopped. She turned, dashed back, and gave me a hug so tight it made me gasp. She kissed my cheek, then ran off.

I stared after her, too stunned to move.

Meatball whined and looked up at me.

"This is too bizarre. What's wrong with her?" I looked back at Sara and Justin's apartment. Something weird was going on with them, too. It couldn't be a coincidence that Justin was hunting around the castle, and now rare items belonging to the family showed up at an auction.

I needed to find out what was going on. And if Alice wouldn't help me, I'd find someone who would.

I pulled out my phone again and dialed a number. "Rupert. I need your help to catch a thief."

❧❧❧❧❧ ❦❦❦❦❦

"I don't like this," Campbell said for about the tenth time that evening. "Using Lord Rupert puts him at risk."

Rupert stood in front of me, smoothing his hands down his perfectly ironed shirt. "I'll be fine. I can look after myself. And you'll both be here to keep an eye on things."

Campbell frowned at me. "I should just bring Justin and Sara in for questioning."

I shook my head. "I only found out what they've been up to because I snuck into their apartment. I basically broke in. I'd get in trouble if that information got out."

Campbell shrugged. "Sacrifices have to be made to serve the greater good."

I glared at Campbell. He'd do it as well.

"We can't let Holly get in trouble. She's discovered a possible crime. A crime your security team didn't pick up on," Rupert said.

I grinned at him. "You're so right. Campbell, what have you been doing that's kept you so busy you missed the coins being taken?"

"Trying to solve two murders."

My grin faded. "I've been thinking about the murders all day. These thefts could be linked to the killings. Bluebell and Herbert found out what Justin and Sara were doing, so they silenced them."

"But Sara seems so nice," Rupert said.

I pursed my lips. "We all know how nice you think she is. You almost asked her out."

His cheeks flushed. "That … that was a misunderstanding. And I only said that to make …"

"What? To make what?" I said.

"Holly, focus!" Campbell said. "The murders. The stolen coins. It makes sense they're connected."

I nodded, turning my attention away from Rupert, who refused to meet my gaze. "It does."

"We need to know how the auctioneers acquired the coins," Rupert said.

"I'm working on that, but they're proving difficult," Campbell said.

"They're proving difficult because they don't want to lose a big commission when they sell the stolen goods from the castle," I said. "That's why they won't tell you who put them up for sale."

"They'll talk. Especially if they think they could be mixed up in two murders," Campbell said.

"And you really think their relationship has been faked?" Rupert said.

I nodded. "I showed Campbell the inside of their apartment. Someone's been sleeping on the couch. And now I think about it, Sara treated Justin more like an annoying brother than a boyfriend. I've never seen them kiss."

"Public displays of affection aren't for everyone, but I agree with Holly," Campbell said.

"They've been lying to us," I said.

"Do you think Justin is the killer?" Rupert said.

"One step at a time. First of all, we need to prove their relationship is fake. Once we've done that, it'll show their alibis are unreliable. And when we've got that information, it could be enough to make one of them crack."

"I still don't like this," Campbell said.

"You don't need to like it, but it'll work. Rupert's already been flirting with Sara, so it won't seem strange that he's asked her to meet with him this evening."

"No, you've got it the wrong way around," Rupert said. "I haven't been flirting with Sara. She's always been friendly with me. She approached me the first day of the project and suggested we meet up one evening. I was flattered, but I didn't think much of it."

"Sara's been coming on to you this whole time?" I said, trying not to feel ridiculously pleased that Rupert hadn't been chasing Sara after all.

"That's right." His expression was earnest as he nodded at me.

My grin returned. "That only adds weight to the idea their relationship is fake."

"Do you think they're both in on this?" Rupert said.

"That's what you need to find out. And it's why we need to do this." I glanced over at Campbell. "Don't you agree?"

He scowled at me, but then nodded. "At the first sign of trouble, I'm stopping this."

"Of course. But we need to get Sara to show her hand, and I think she trusts me," Rupert said.

I checked the time. "We have to hide. Sara will be here in a few minutes. You know what you have to do?"

Rupert nodded. "I'll flirt with her and see how she responds. If she's interested, I'll push on the question of her relationship with Justin."

"Perfect. You'll be great." I patted his arm. "All set, Campbell?"

He walked over to the tall cabinet in the corner of the room we'd cleared out an hour ago. He opened the door and gestured for me to go inside.

I stepped over the edge and settled in the corner. Campbell followed.

Rupert closed the door behind us, leaving a tiny gap that we could peer out of.

Campbell nudged me to the side. "I have to be able to see this."

"So do I! And I can read people's body language. I'll know if Rupert's at risk."

"You won't. And I've been trained by top military experts to read body language."

"I'm innately attuned to it. Training can't beat that."

Campbell sighed. "Kneel down. You look out the bottom, and I'll stand over you."

I didn't love that option, but it meant we both got to watch. I crouched, trying to get comfortable on the hard base of the cabinet.

Campbell shuffled into position over me, leaning forward and staring out of the crack.

I grimaced and crouched lower, glad no one could see us in this odd position.

Rupert paced the room. I wanted to go out and tell him not to be so nervous or he'd give the game away. But Rupert always lived on his nerves. If he appeared too debonair and suave, Sara would know something was going on.

We only had to wait a couple of minutes before footsteps approached the room.

There was a light tap on the door. "Rupert, it's Sara."

"Come in." He glanced over at the cabinet before hurrying to the main door and pulling it open.

"I wasn't sure I was in the right place. There are so many rooms in the castle that it's easy to get lost." Sara giggled. She wore a long dark red dress with a revealing neckline. "Thanks for inviting me for a drink. I'd almost given up on asking you out."

"I'm glad you didn't. I've got some wine. I hope that's okay."

"Sure. I love wine."

I peeked through the gap in the cabinet. Sara was walking slowly around the room inspecting everything.

"This room is amazing. It's like another world. The antiques are so beautiful." She turned and smiled at Rupert.

He handed her a glass of red wine. "It's a great place."

"And one day, you'll be in charge of all of this." She raised her glass. "That's something to look forward to."

"It's a big responsibility, a place like this." Rupert glanced at the cabinet again.

"He needs to stop doing that," Campbell muttered. "He'll give us away."

I shushed him and kept on listening.

"You don't need to do anything other than employ loads of people to deal with the boring stuff," Sara said. "You get to have all the fun and live in this incredible place."

"Yes, I suppose that's true. Do you have a place of your own?"

She shook her head. "I just rent a room. I move around a lot for work. But I'm willing to settle for the right person."

Rupert cleared his throat. "You're an attractive woman. You must have lots of men interested in you."

She laughed. "You're sweet. They're not exactly beating down my door, but I do okay. How about you?"

"Um, how about me?"

"You're one of the most eligible bachelors in this country. You must have considered looking for that special someone. If the gossip magazines have it right, you're single."

"Yes! Um, yes, I am. But one day I plan to marry."

"If you're looking for someone who's fun, available, and loves history, you could do worse than me." Sara fluttered her lashes.

"That's flattering," Rupert said. "But I have to ask, aren't you in a relationship with Justin?"

Sara took a long sip of wine before setting down the glass. "Not really. Justin's a great guy, but it's nothing serious." She caught hold of Rupert's hand. "I'm looking for the right one. Just like you."

"And Justin isn't the right one?"

"He's a friend."

"I thought you were sharing the same apartment?"

"Have you been checking up on me, Lord Rupert?" Sara giggled again. "I didn't know you were that interested in me. Are you jealous that I'm with Justin?"

"Maybe. I wouldn't want to share you with anyone else."

"You're so adorable. Let me put your mind at rest. Justin and I are friends. Nothing's ever happened between us. He's a nice guy, but I'm not interested in him in that way."

"And you're not intimately acquainted with him?"

"If that's your upper class way of asking if we're sleeping together, then the answer is no. We're sharing an apartment, but Justin takes the couch every night. He gave me the only bed in the place. That's it. I'm totally single, and totally yours if you want me."

Rupert looked at the cabinet again. "I … That's great news. Maybe we—"

Sara threw herself at Rupert, grabbed his face, and landed a kiss on his lips.

Campbell grabbed my arm. "Stay where you are."

"She's kissing him! That's the proof we needed that she lied." My hand went to the door. I wasn't prone to violence, but I wanted to punch Sara. No one got to kiss Rupert.

"I can see that. That doesn't give you a reason to attack her."

I gritted my teeth, jealousy boiling inside me as Sara plastered herself against Rupert and continued to kiss him.

Rupert stood with his arms by his sides and his eyes wide open.

"Relax." Sara pulled back and smiled up at him. "We're not doing anything wrong. And you did invite me here. I know you didn't want to show off your wine collection. Let's have some fun. Get to know each other."

The door to the room slammed open. Justin stood there, glaring at Sara.

Chapter 21

"What are you doing?" Justin strode into the room.

Sara stepped back from Rupert, her cheeks growing pink. "I thought you were staying in to do research."

"And you said you were going for a walk. I knew something was up when you put on that dress and all that make-up. Most of which is now smeared on Lord Rupert. I got suspicious, so I followed you." Justin glared at Sara.

She crossed her arms over her chest. "I saw an opportunity."

Rupert cleared his throat. "I didn't mean to cause any problems. I didn't realize—"

"Ignore Justin," Sara said. "He's obsessed with me. He won't take a hint. Justin, we're just friends."

"No, we're supposed to be in a relationship," Justin said. "Why are you kissing him?"

"Not now. We can talk about this another time," Sara said.

Justin shook his head. "No way. We're together. We're doing this together."

Sara gestured at Rupert. "But I have a lord interested in me. You'd behave just the same if Princess Alice came on to you."

"I should leave," Rupert said.

Sara grabbed his arm. "You're not going anywhere. We're just getting to know each other. Justin, you're leaving. Go now. Don't mess this up for me."

"We're partners. We had our future mapped out."

"We can still have a great future. Just not the way we'd planned." Sara waved a hand between them. "This was never a permanent arrangement."

Justin's mouth fell open. "You're messing everything up."

"I'm sorry about this, Lord Rupert." Sara stalked over to Justin and pushed him back. "Go away. I'll find you later. We'll figure things out. Everything will be fine."

"You're not ditching me for this guy. We had a deal." Justin grabbed Sara's hand.

She yanked it loose. "The deal's changed. Get lost."

"Should we get out now?" I whispered to Campbell.

"Let's give them one more minute. They're digging themselves a nice, big hole. We just need one of them to say something incriminating about the coins or the killings, and we've got them."

Sara looked at Rupert. "Can't you get your security to deal with this idiot?"

"You'd better watch what you're saying," Justin said. "I'm not an idiot."

She sighed. "Fine. You're not an idiot. But I'm on a date. You're only embarrassing yourself by staying here."

"I'm the one embarrassing myself! You were just climbing up Lord Rupert and inspecting his fillings with your tongue," Justin said.

"Steady on," Rupert said. "Everyone calm down."

Sara shrieked as Justin lunged at her. He swung a punch, and it landed on Rupert's jaw.

Campbell crashed out of the cabinet at the same time as me. He charged over and tackled Justin to the floor.

Sara screamed and backed away. "What's going on? Why were you both hiding in the cabinet?"

I hurried over to Rupert and touched his jaw. "Are you okay?"

He shook his head as he blinked his eyes. "I'm not sure. I didn't see the punch coming. Was he aiming at me?"

"Of course I was aiming at you. Keep away from Sara. We had everything planned, and you've ruined it." Justin yelped as Campbell dragged him to his feet.

Sara's bottom jaw wobbled. "I don't understand. What are you all doing here?"

"Tell us about the Audley gold coins," I said to her. "Which one of you stole them?"

They were both silent as they stared at each other.

"We know it was one of you," I said. "We've been in touch with the auctioneers. They confirmed they received the coins."

"I know nothing about that," Sara said. "We're only here to work on the restoration project."

"Is that right, Justin?" I said. "You haven't been researching the history of Audley Castle because you want to find treasures to steal and sell?"

Justin opened his mouth, his gaze on Sara.

"He knows nothing," Sara said. "Neither of us do."

He nodded. "That's right."

It was easy to see who was in charge of this fake relationship.

"Did you put him up to it?" I said to Sara. "You learned about the coins and convinced Justin to steal them for you."

Sara looked at Justin and narrowed her eyes, but she didn't say anything. She turned her attention to Rupert. "Has this been a setup, or are you really interested in me?"

Rupert took a step back, his hand on his bruised jaw. "We needed to know the truth. We figured out you'd been lying about your relationship with Justin. We had to get proof of that."

"This is a honey trap?" Sara barked out a laugh.

"It is," I said. "And you fell right in. You were quick enough to ditch Justin and jump into Rupert's arms at the first opportunity you got."

"Because he likes me. Lord Rupert is always flirting with me. I was hardly going to reject him. He lives in this enormous castle and is worth a fortune."

"And you figured Rupert could give you much more than Justin, even after you'd pocketed the money from selling the stolen coins," I said.

"I don't care who's dating who. You'll both go to prison. But whoever talks first will get the lighter sentence," Campbell said.

I sucked in a breath and looked at Sara and then Justin to see who would crack under pressure.

Justin heaved out a sigh. "I told you those coins were a mistake."

"Be quiet. Stop talking," Sara said.

Justin sagged in Campbell's grip. "This is Sara's fault. She got greedy."

Everyone turned their attention to Sara.

Her face went red, she pressed her lips together, and scowled at Justin. "I'm greedy! You're the one obsessed with that ridiculous chalice. It doesn't exist, but that's all you're interested in. The second you knew we were coming to Audley Castle, you wouldn't shut up about it."

"The Audley chalice?" Rupert said. "That hasn't been around for a long time. It disappeared a few hundred years ago."

"It's still here. I'm sure of it," Justin said. "I've been researching it for months. I found an inventory log that alluded to the chalice. It was dated less than fifty years ago."

"That can't be true," Rupert said. "We do an inventory of the castle every year. It's never shown up."

"And it wouldn't," Justin said. "It's not on display."

"You're an idiot," Sara said. "You had to keep snooping around and making people suspicious."

"Because the chalice is worth a fortune," Justin said.

"It may be worth a fortune, but it's not yours," I said. "What were you planning to do with the chalice when you found it?"

"He didn't know," Sara said with a derisive snort. "He was living some stupid fantasy."

"It wasn't a fantasy. The Audley Castle chalice is special. It was created using magic," Justin said.

Campbell huffed out a laugh. "A magic chalice. What do you think this place is, King Arthur's court?"

"You see. He's a fool," Sara said. "It comes from playing too many online fantasy games. He thinks he's on a hero quest. Find the gold chalice and be gifted a prize."

"The only prize both of you will get is prison time," Campbell said.

Justin licked his lips, while Sara continued to glare at him.

"I've done the research," Justin said. "I was so close to finding it. Then Sara decided to change the plans."

"My plan was never to chase after something that wasn't real," Sara said.

"But when you heard you were coming here to work, it was too good of an opportunity to miss," I said. "Did you take this job specifically to rob the family?"

"Don't act like you haven't thought about taking something from this place. You work here every day. You're surrounded by things that cost more than ten years of your salary. Don't you get tempted? You could do so much with the money. These old families hoard wealth. It's wrong. We deserve some of that. The work we do is valuable. There's never enough funding for restoration projects."

"You were stealing from the family to fund your work?" Campbell said.

"Of course she wasn't," Justin said. "Sara's greedy and shallow. She wanted to buy a place in Antigua and spend her days hanging out on the beach. She cares nothing about conservation."

"And you do? Oh, my mistake, all you care about is made up artifacts and chasing things that aren't real," Sara said.

"You chasing after Lord Rupert is hardly real," Justin said. "Did you seriously think he liked you? Who's the bigger fool now?"

Sara snarled at him. "This was all Justin's doing. He learned about the project, convinced me to fake a relationship with him, and planned out what we were going to steal."

"You're lying! This was your idea. I'd been out of work for three months and was desperate. You came to me. You told me what you wanted to do. I had no other option. I was months behind on my bills and about to get thrown out of my lodgings."

"We'll know soon enough which one of you contacted the auctioneers about the stolen coins," Campbell said. "They're cooperating with us."

"And whoever it was, it makes sense that you also killed Bluebell and Herbert," I said.

Sara sucked in a breath.

"What? No, that's not true," Justin said.

"Did they find out what you were doing?" I said. "Did Bluebell get suspicious and confront you?"

"That wasn't me," Justin said. "I never had a problem with Bluebell."

"Well, don't blame me," Sara said. "Herbert killed her."

"I don't think he did. Bluebell found out you'd stolen the gold coins and insisted you return them." I turned to Sara. "And I don't think Justin killed her. He's scared of heights."

"That's right! I am. I never go on the scaffolding," Justin said. "It wasn't me. I'm innocent."

"You're saying it was Sara?" Campbell said.

Justin blinked several times and swallowed.

"No! I'm not taking the fall for this. This was all Justin's idea."

"What was?" I said.

Sara let out a long, shaky breath. "He said to steal the coins."

"As a joke!" Justin said. "I didn't mean it. Then you came back with all the books and the layout of the castle. You said we should do it. It would change our lives."

"That was all you," Sara said. "Don't be fooled by him. Justin's mean. He forced me to help him. I was scared for my life."

"Sara, why are you doing this to me? We're supposed to be partners."

"Because you're a killer. You killed Herbert."

Justin jabbed a finger at her. "And you killed Bluebell. You never liked her. When she found out about the coins, you had to get rid of her."

They glared at each other.

"That sounded like a confession," Campbell said.

"No! I confessed to nothing," Justin said. "Herbert was being irrational. Ever since Bluebell died, he was a mess."

"That's no reason to kill him," I said.

"He had no choice," Sara said. "Herbert caught him searching the castle for that dumb chalice. And he was foolish enough to ask Herbert's advice. He asked him where he could sell something like that."

"It's not a dumb chalice," Justin muttered.

"But you were interested in more than the chalice," I said. "I read the books you loaned me. All the sections about the antiques and valuables in the castle had been well-read and several sections highlighted."

"I … that means nothing. I enjoy research, that's all," Justin said.

"Herbert caught on to what Justin was doing. He fired him. He said he couldn't be trusted," Sara said.

"I'd have quit anyway," Justin said. "I was sick of this place. And now you've shown your true colors, I'm sick of you, too." He glared at me. "You haven't got any evidence that I killed Herbert. You're just guessing."

"When I was chasing you after you killed Herbert," I said, "Meatball grabbed hold of the leg of your pants. If we search your apartment, we'll find the torn clothing. There'll be evidence on that."

Justin's face paled. "I often damage my clothes working on site. I have holes in most of my clothes."

"We'll also have Sara's statement, if she's willing to cooperate," Campbell said.

Justin gulped and turned a pleading expression to Sara.

"What's in it for me if I do?" Sara said.

"I'll put in a good word for you. See if your sentence can be reduced," Campbell said.

"That's not good enough. I'm not going to prison."

"That can't be avoided. You killed someone. But if you cooperate, that'll be looked on favorably by the judge," Campbell said.

"Sara, don't you dare. We're in this together. You said we'd stick with each other until the end."

Sara sighed. "The end has come. And I'm done covering for you. I'll give a statement. Justin killed Bluebell and Herbert."

"No! Not Bluebell. I could never go up on the scaffolding. That's the truth. Ask anyone. I slipped once when I was working on a painting. I was hanging by my tether for several minutes before anyone came to help me. I shake if someone even asks me to climb a ladder. I've even had therapy to cure my fear of heights. Nothing helps. I didn't do it."

"But you killed Herbert," I said. "You lied about your relationship with Sara so you'd both have alibis. That made it easier for you to move around the castle. And you stole from the Audley family."

Justin's forehead wrinkled, and he scraped a hand down his face. "It wasn't fair. I didn't deserve to be fired. I tried to make Herbert understand, but he wouldn't listen. He said if the chalice was ever found, it would be returned to the family. What's the point of that? It's lost to them, and they don't care enough to find it. I do. Having that chalice would have changed our lives." His shoulders slumped. "Well, I was hoping to make a life with Sara, until I realized how evil and greedy she was."

"This is your fault. If you hadn't made the suggestion about stealing the coins, I'd have never even thought about it. Justin's the one who should be arrested," Sara said.

"You're both being arrested," Campbell said.

Sara tensed, then bolted for the door.

Rupert chased after her. He caught hold of her shoulder. She spun around, shoved him away, and yanked the door open.

Two members of Campbell's security team stood outside.

She shrieked in rage. "I'm only trying to make a better life for myself. You have all of this. The Audley family are the greedy ones. They should share. And Bluebell was such an uptight harpy. She threatened me. She said I'd lose my job. I had to stop that from happening."

"Sara, you got caught out. You must pay for that," Rupert said.

She scowled as the security guys caught hold of her.

Campbell marched out with Justin and handed him over to his team. "Call the police. Tell them we found Bluebell and Herbert's killers." He walked along the corridor a few paces as he conferred with his men.

I turned to Rupert. "You did great! We solved the murders."

His faint smile suggested all was not well.

"Is your jaw hurting?"

"A bit. It's not that. I didn't expect Sara to kiss me. One second, we were talking, and the next she threw herself at me. I didn't know what to do. I didn't think I should push her away because it would have looked strange. I hope you didn't mind watching me kiss another woman."

I had minded. I'd minded a lot. I had no clue how I'd figure this out, but I wanted Rupert to myself. He may be a lord, and I may be a kitchen assistant, but there had to be a solution to this problem.

"I'm just glad we caught Sara and Justin. They fooled me. I didn't see them as killers," I said.

"Neither did I." Rupert's forehead wrinkled as he watched Sara and Justin get led along the corridor. "But did you mind that I kissed Sara?"

I bit my bottom lip. "Technically, she kissed you."

"Yes! But I want to know what you think about that." The look of intensity in his eyes made my heart race.

I clasped my hands together. He wasn't letting this go, and I couldn't be a coward and ignore it. "Rupert, we've been friends for a while, haven't we?"

"Yes. I value your friendship. I enjoy having you here. I'm always telling you that the castle wouldn't be the same if you weren't here."

"Thanks. I feel that it's my home. And although I don't want things to change, I think they need to."

"What changes do you think need to be made? You don't want to leave me? I mean, the castle."

I looked up at him. I knew what I wanted, but I had no clue how to get it.

Campbell appeared in the doorway. "Holly, you need to come with me. The police will want our statements."

I sighed. "I'd better go. Are you sure you're okay?"

"I'm great. But you were saying about change?" Rupert said.

"Holly, get a move on," Campbell said.

I stepped toward Rupert, but then backed away just as fast. There were loose ends in this murder to tidy up. Now wasn't the time to go declaring my feelings.

But if I didn't do it soon, I never would.

Chapter 22

I smoothed down my smart black dress as I stood in front of the mirror in my bedroom. It had been a day since Sara and Justin had been arrested for Bluebell and Herbert's murder. They were still bickering over who'd planned the murders, but the Audley coins had been recovered from the auctioneer, and the police were preparing to charge them both with murder. Everything seemed back to normal.

Well, almost everything.

I was about to meet Rupert and find out why he wanted a private audience with me.

There was a knock on my bedroom door. I turned just as Gran opened it.

"You look lovely, Holly," Gran said. "Lady Philippa's here."

"She is? Does she need something?"

"I don't think so. She came for a visit. We've gotten friendly these last few months. And she wants to hear about the murders."

I did a final check of my make-up and headed into the kitchen. Lady Philippa was sitting at the kitchen table, a mug of coffee and a plate of cookies in front of her.

She smiled up at me. "You look adorable. It's a perfect dress for the occasion."

"What occasion is that?" I said.

Gran cleared her throat. "I was just catching Lady Philippa up on the excitement you've been having. Hiding in closets, listening to confessions, stopping the family treasure being taken. What an adventure."

"Oh, yes. It was a crazy few days. Sara and Justin will go away for a long time."

Lady Philippa couldn't seem to stop smiling. "I'm still in shock that they stole the Audley family coins. How did they know where to find them?"

"Justin and Sara are excellent researchers. They found a plan of the castle rooms and have been methodically searching them." I reached for a cookie, but Gran slapped the back of my hand.

"You don't want cookie crumbs down the front of your nice dress."

"But I'm hungry."

"They'll be here when you come back," Gran said. She shared a smile with Lady Philippa. They were up to something.

"I heard the killers were also looking for the missing family chalice," Lady Philippa said.

"Apparently so. It was Justin's obsession." I looked longingly at the plate of forbidden cookies.

"It all makes sense now. I kept dreaming about a rare lost bowl. That must have been the chalice Justin wanted to get his grubby little hands on," Lady Philippa said. "My ghosts were most concerned that he'd find it and take it away."

Gran opened her mouth, but I beat her to it.

"Do your spirit friends have any idea where this missing chalice is?"

"No. Well, they could. They can pass through walls, so they see everything. If they do, they're not telling me."

I glanced around the kitchen. "They don't come out this way, do they? I really don't want an unexpected guest arriving while I'm taking a bath."

Lady Philippa chuckled. "They prefer the castle. You have nothing to worry about."

Gran loudly cleared her throat and nudged me. "It's time for you to go."

I checked the time and tried not to frown. "Yes, I do need to get going."

"Excellent." Lady Philippa stood.

"I'll walk back with you, shall I?" I said to her.

"I'll come too," Gran said.

"You want to walk to the castle with me?" I said.

"I could do with the fresh air." Gran's eyes twinkled.

"You've been outside with Ray for most of the day."

Gran busied herself with attaching Saffron's leash. "And this little one needs a stroll."

I shrugged. "Okay. Let me get Meatball ready."

"He's all set. I put his little walking sock on his sore paw. Everyone must be there," Lady Philippa said.

"Be where?" I said.

She clapped her hands together and grinned. "We can't say."

Gran bustled Lady Philippa to the door. "Let's take a nice evening walk, and then you can meet with the lovely Lord Rupert."

"He's such a charming young man. Although I'm biased," Lady Philippa said. "Hurry, Holly. We don't want you to be late."

"Let me grab the trolley. I don't want Meatball walking all that way," I said.

Gran pulled open the front door. Ray was outside, attending to the beautiful plush pink rose bushes by the apartment door.

She strode over and kissed him on the cheek. "You should come with us. We're taking an evening stroll."

"Don't mind if I do," Ray said. "Good evening, Lady Philippa, Holly. It's a nice night for it." He looked very smart for someone who'd been gardening all day. He wore a clean white shirt and a suit jacket over a pair of dark jeans.

"It's the perfect evening," Lady Philippa said.

I set up the trolley and placed Meatball in it. It was the perfect evening for weirdness. But I couldn't dwell on their odd behavior. I still didn't know what I was going to say to Rupert. Or more importantly, what he had planned for me.

I hadn't seen him all day, despite sending him a couple of messages to make sure he was doing okay after being molested by Sara.

Alice was also ignoring my messages, but I was used to that. Even though I didn't like it, I had to accept she no longer wanted me in her life.

"Stop dawdling, Holly. You don't want to keep Lord Rupert waiting," Gran said.

I picked up the pace as I pulled the trolley, my ankle barely causing me any trouble.

I petted Meatball on the head as he sat up, watching the world go by. "Your paw will soon be back to normal, and then we can go on nice long walks again."

"Rupert loves long walks," Lady Philippa said. "I'm sure he'd like to come with you."

"We can go walking together any time he likes," I said.

Lady Philippa sighed. "That's perfect. Everything is perfect."

We reached the castle, and I turned to everyone. "Enjoy the rest of your walk."

"We're coming in with you," Gran said.

Lady Philippa nodded. "Of course."

I placed my hands on my hips. "Wait, a minute. What's going on? Why are you all here? Why is Lady Philippa so excited? And Ray, why are you wearing smart clothes?"

Ray adjusted his shirt collar. "Your Gran thought it would be a good idea."

"A good idea for what?"

"Hurry on in," Lady Philippa said. "You don't want to keep Rupert waiting."

"Go!" Gran gave me a gentle push. "We'll be right behind you."

"He's in the royal suite," Lady Philippa said.

"He is? I've never been in there."

"Now's your chance."

Gran flapped her hands at me. "Go!"

I had no choice but to head along the corridor to the royal suite. I smoothed down my dress again and knocked on the door.

It was flung open by Alice.

"Um, hi! Are you going to slam the door in my face again?"

"Don't be silly. Get in here." She grabbed me and yanked me inside.

I took a few seconds to look around the room. It was huge, with high ceilings, chandeliers, a giant marble fireplace, and elegant furnishings in shades of cream and gold.

"Where's Rupert?" I said.

"He'll be here soon." Alice bounced on her toes. "I'm so glad you came."

"I had no choice. I got summoned."

She smacked my arm. "It wasn't a summons. It was an invitation."

"I didn't know you would be here." I glanced at her. "Are we still friends?"

"Of course. And so much more. Do you like the room?"

"It's stunning. Just like the rest of the castle."

"Only family members come in here."

"I know. That's why I was surprised when Lady Philippa said this was where I was meeting Rupert."

"Oh! Granny. I almost forgot." Alice dashed to the door and pulled it open. "Come in, everyone."

Gran, Lady Philippa, Ray, Meatball, and Saffron walked in.

Ray whistled as he looked around. "Beautiful."

"It's one of my favorite rooms," Alice said.

I caught hold of her arm. "What is everyone doing here?"

"I invited them."

"Okay, and I have no problem with that. This is your home. It's just that Rupert said he wanted a private audience in here with me. This is the opposite of private."

Alice checked the time. "Where is my brother? He can't be late this evening. If he doesn't hurry up, I'll start without him."

"Start what?"

"Just you wait. It's so exciting, I'm almost ready to burst," Alice said.

Rupert walked into the room. He looked a little startled as he took in everyone.

"Hurry up," Alice said to him.

He looked dashing in a tailored gray suit and white shirt. "Sorry, I forgot something." He patted his pocket.

"Holly, everyone else, gather around the table. I've got something important to show you." Alice grabbed my hand and pulled me to her side as everybody assembled around the gold-trimmed table in the center of the room.

"What's going on?" I whispered to her.

"You'll know in a minute." She looked around the group and smiled. "I've been researching family trees. I've been trying to get Holly to do hers for ages, but she's not that interested."

"It's not that. I just get busy with other things."

"Usually solving murders," Lady Philippa said.

"Sometimes," I said.

Alice squeaked and giggled. "So, I did your family tree for you."

"I know. I found it in the apartment. I haven't had a chance to take a good look at it, though."

"Then you missed a surprise," Alice said. "And so did I, at first. It wasn't until Rupert mentioned the name Baron Mistelthorpe that it jogged my memory. I went back and had another look. When I figured it out, I got all tingly with excitement."

"What gave you the tingles?" I said.

Alice sucked in a deep breath. "Holly Holmes. You're descended from royalty."

"Not quite," Lady Philippa said. "But you are descended from an old and noble family."

Gran smiled. "I knew we came from grand roots."

"Who am I descended from? I've never heard of anyone noble in the family line," I said.

"Let me show you." Alice pointed at the family tree. "Baron Mistelthorpe had three illegitimate children that we know of. One of them was a relative of yours."

I peered at the elaborate family tree. "Which is nice, but I don't know why you're getting so excited about that?"

Alice hugged me tightly. "Because you have noble connections. You come from an ancient and well-respected family."

I hugged her back, but then shook my head and stepped away. "Those connections are ancient, though. And you're overlooking the illegitimate part. That's got to mean something. A child out of marriage wasn't something people approved of a few hundred years ago."

"To some families it will, but not this one. The Mistelthorpes honor their connections. I've been in touch with them and showed them the family tree. They're excited to meet a relative."

"Alice, I don't know. They're not my family. Not really." I looked at Gran.

She smiled and nodded.

"They absolutely are," Alice said. "And best of all, they want you recognized."

"As what?"

"A Mistelthorpe."

"Um, I don't know. I'm fine with being a Holmes. It's who I am."

Alice pinched my arm. "You don't have to change your name. But they want to meet you and show everyone you're a part of their family."

"It's not as if you have much family left, Holly," Gran said. "Your dad's no longer with us, and although you have your step-mom and half-sister, it's not the same thing. You've only got me. And I'm always letting you down."

"That's not true. You've never let me down." I shook my head. "What do you make of all this?"

"It's incredible." Gran's smile broadened. "Especially if you get your own castle. I can have a turret just like Lady Philippa."

"I won't get a castle, will I?" I said to Alice.

"No, you're not about to come into lots of money. What this means is you'll be formally accepted into this noble family. And even better, it means you can come to all the social events with me." She hugged me again. "Balls, banquets, and dancing will be so much fun with you by my side."

I squirmed out of her grip. I didn't know what to think. I stared around at everyone. They all seemed happy for me.

"Well, I guess this is good. But I don't want anything to change. I like my life here. I love my job as a kitchen assistant, and I love my gran. I don't mind meeting the Mistelthorpes, and we can talk about family trees and distant relatives, but I can't see how anything else will be different."

"It will. Trust me. Names matter in our social circle." Alice gestured at everyone to move away from the table. "Now, it's time to leave Holly and Rupert to talk." She bustled the group to the other side of the room, where they settled on couches and chairs, clearly still able to hear us.

Rupert cleared his throat several times before taking my hand.

I stared up at him. "Is this why Alice has been so weird?"

He nodded. "Yes. She didn't want to say anything before it was verified. She wanted to be certain the family connection was real."

"I still don't see how that matters. It's not going to change anything for me."

Rupert patted his pocket again, and his grip on my hand tightened. "Don't you see, it does. Holly, I've always thought highly of you. You're the sweetest, smartest, prettiest woman I've ever met."

I swallowed, my cheeks growing warm. "Thanks. I think you're great, too."

"You put up with my clumsiness, my love of poetry, my last-minute demands for sweet treats from the kitchen. You never complain. You're always happy. Always willing to help."

"Sure. But that is sort of my job."

"Get on with it," Alice hissed.

Rupert ignored her. "Holly, my life changed when you came into it. I was having a nice time, drifting along, not having any direction. You showed me that sometimes you have to take risks. You put yourself in danger all the time to help other people solve problems."

I huffed out a laugh, my heart beating fast. "Campbell would tell you I was being nosy."

"Well, curiosity is no bad thing." Rupert patted his pocket again. "What I'm trying to say is you make me happy. I don't want you going anywhere, and I know one day you will. You'll outgrow the castle, and someone will snap you up and whisk you away for an incredible life."

"Only in my wildest dreams."

"Oh! You want to leave the castle?"

"No! Of course I don't. But that sort of thing doesn't happen, not really." I let out a sigh. "I'm happy to hear you don't want me to leave. I thought you didn't want me around anymore. When you said you wanted a private audience with me, I got it into my head that you were going to sack me."

"That couldn't be further from the truth. I want you to stay at the castle forever," Rupert said.

"What about your dad's plans to expand your estate in another country?"

"He's doing that because he's worried I'm not settling down. He thinks I have no focus. I don't want to run another estate. This is my home. Just as it is yours."

"Rupert, I'll do it myself if you don't hurry up," Alice said.

Rupert closed his eyes for a second. He opened them, and the intensity in his gaze made me gasp.

He knelt on one knee and looked up at me. "So, Holly Holmes, I would like to ask—"

Meatball gamboled over. He bounced on Rupert, knocking him off balance, and sending him to the floor. He jumped on him and licked his face. Saffron raced over and joined in the fun.

Alice groaned. "This wouldn't have happened if my brother wasn't such a slow poke. We're all getting bored waiting."

"Meatball, no!" I scooped him up and held him in my arms.

Rupert staggered upright and back onto his knees.

Gran hurried over and collected a yapping Saffron before dashing back to the couch.

"Sorry. Meatball gets excited when people are on the floor. He thinks you want to play with him," I said.

Rupert chuckled as he wiped dog slobber off his face. "And I wouldn't have it any other way. So, Holly and Meatball, I think you're both wonderful. I want you in my life, and I don't want you going anywhere. Your home is here, with me."

"And with me," Alice said.

"Of course, unfortunately, you know the rest of my family. They're a part of the package," he said.

I wasn't sure I could speak, but I gave it a try. "Rupert, what are you trying to ask me?"

He caught hold of my hand again. "One simple question. Holly, will you marry me?"

There were several gasps from the other side of the room, but I kept my gaze fixed to Rupert. "Marriage?"

"Yes. I want you to be my wife."

I adjusted my grip on Meatball. He licked my cheek and wagged his tail, suggesting he liked the idea.

I stared down at Rupert. I really had lost the power of speech. This wasn't what I'd been expecting.

"This is where you say yes," Alice stage whispered.

I looked over at the group. Everyone was leaning forward in their seats, awaiting my answer.

I returned my attention to Rupert. "No. I won't marry you."

His eyes widened, and his face paled.

Alice gasped, and a sob shot out of her mouth.

Then everyone started talking at once.

"Stop! Let me finish." I tugged on Rupert's hand to make him stand. "I also like you very much. I'm fond of you. And seeing you kissing Sara, I didn't like it. I want to be the one kissing you, but I never thought it would happen. We're too far apart. You're in fancy twinkly, high-class circles of refinement, and I'm a flour and buttercream covered nosy kitchen assistant. They don't seem to fit together."

"That's not true. It could work. It—"

"Wait! I'm saying no, because we've never even had a proper date."

"We have. I've taken you for coffee. And we painted those pots together. And we go on lots of walks."

I smiled. "Yes, they were sort of dates. But why don't we do this properly? And I need time to get used to the fact I come from some noble family I've never heard of, and they want to meet me. I need to figure out what that means."

"You do want to go out with me?" Rupert said. "Holly, I'd marry you tomorrow if you let me."

"That's sweet of you. But let's take it slow. We'll go on some dates, I'll get used to this new information, and we'll take it from there."

"Yes, I'd like that," Rupert said. "Now, if I may, I'd really like to kiss you."

I glanced at the waiting group. "Let's do that when it's just the two of us, shall we?"

He leaned down and gave me a sweet kiss on the cheek. "Of course. Anything to make you happy."

I set Meatball on the ground just as Alice raced over and gave me another bear hug. "I'm so angry with you for turning down my brother."

"It's not a hard no, it's a soft maybe."

She laughed. "I wanted to start wedding planning right away. It doesn't matter, we can do it anyway and just pretend you said yes. Because you will, won't you?"

"Alice, that's between me and Rupert," I said.

"And I'm not letting you near our wedding," Rupert said. "You don't know the first thing about planning one. You'd probably have it unicorn themed and everything would be covered in sparkles."

"There's nothing wrong with either of those things," Alice said. "I'll do whatever Holly wants."

I gave her a warning pinch on the arm. "We can discuss weddings another time, when I've recovered from my shock."

Everyone else walked over, smiling and congratulating us.

I caught hold of Rupert's hand and gave it a squeeze, still dizzy from all these revelations. Rupert wanted to marry me. And I think I wanted to marry him, but I'd only ever daydreamed about it. Now it was real.

Things would be very different around Audley Castle from now on. I had noble connections and a lord for a boyfriend.

Gran tugged me to one side. "Is everything good, Holly?"

"After I've had about a year to process all this, I'm sure I'll be fine."

She chuckled. "I always knew there was something special about you."

"You're going to have to help me through this. I have no clue how to behave like a lady."

"Of course. We're in this together. Now, go spend time with your handsome new boyfriend." She gave me a gentle nudge back to Rupert.

I looked over at the open door. Campbell stood there. He grinned at me and nodded.

He knew about this and didn't tell me? Why wasn't I surprised? I'd missed all the hints he'd dropped, but I'd been so focused on the murders that I'd missed the mystery going on right under my nose.

Rupert adored me, and I adored him right back. The rest we'd have to figure out with the support of my family. Old and new.

About Author

K.E. O'Connor (Karen) is a cozy mystery author living in the beautiful British countryside. She loves all things mystery, animals, and cake (these often feature in her books.)

When she's not writing about mysteries, murder, and treats, she volunteers at a local animal sanctuary, reads a ton of books, binge watches mystery series on TV, and dreams about living somewhere warmer.

To stay in touch with the fun, clean mysteries, where the killer always gets their just desserts:

Newsletter: www.subscribepage.com/cozymysteries
Website: www.keoconnor.com/writing
Facebook: www.facebook.com/keoconnorauthor

Also By

Enjoy the complete Holly Holmes cozy culinary mysteries in paperback or e-book.

Cream Caramel and Murder
Chocolate Swirls and Murder
Vanilla Whip and Murder
Cherry Cream and Murder
Blueberry Blast and Murder
Mocha Cream and Murder
Lemon Drizzle and Murder
Maple Glaze and Murder
Mint Frosting and Murder

Read on for a peek at book eight in the series - Maple Glaze and Murder!

Chapter 1

I adjusted the lace around my neckline and smoothed the pale fabric of my full-length silk dress. I took a deep breath, and it came out shaky.

I stared at myself in the mirror in my bedroom. I almost didn't recognize the woman staring back at me. My dark hair was shining and had a slight wave to it, and my make-up had been done by an expert, so my eyes looked huge and my mouth glossy. I was more used to flour smeared on my cheek and chocolate on my apron.

Meatball, my beloved corgi cross, sat on my bed, watching my every move. Beside him sat Saffron, my gran's dog. They wore fetching bow ties, Meatball's in black and Saffron's in red, and were ready for the wedding to begin.

I glanced at the large bouquet of cream and yellow flowers waiting for me. "What do you think, pooches? Are we ready to go?"

Saffron gave a little whine, and Meatball wagged his tail.

"This is an important day. Everything needs to go right. We can't let the families down."

Meatball wagged his tail again, and Saffron lifted one paw.

"And it's a big day for both of you. Be on your best behavior when you walk along that aisle. You wouldn't have been picked to be a groomsman or a doggie bridesmaid if I didn't think you could be relied on."

I had no worries about Meatball behaving. He'd be an angel, unless he sniffed out a tasty piece of sausage hidden in someone's pocket. But Saffron was another matter. She could be a stubborn lady when she wanted to be and wasn't a fan of crowds. And there'd be plenty of people at the wedding this afternoon.

I peeked out the window and smiled. It was perfect wedding weather. Fluffy white clouds drifted across a bright blue sky. There was barely any wind, but it wasn't too warm, so I wouldn't sweat in my elegant dress.

The bedroom door behind me burst open, and Princess Alice Audley raced through. She grabbed my hands. "Holly, you look so pretty. Even prettier than me, and I didn't think that was possible." She twirled me, and I laughed.

Alice looked stunning in a green silk gown. Her blonde curls were piled loosely on her head, and a sparkling tiara nestled among them.

"I can't believe this is happening. I'm so excited," she said.

"Me too. But I'm nervous. All those people are waiting in the castle."

"Don't worry about them. They'll only be thinking good thoughts about you when they see you in that dress," Alice said. "But you need to hurry. You can't be late today."

"I'm ready to go," I said. "Did you see Gran when you came in?"

Alice nodded. "She looks twice as nervous as you. Grab your flowers, let's get a move on."

I caught hold of my bouquet, then hurried out of the bedroom, Meatball and Saffron following me. I entered the lounge to find Gran standing by the window staring out of it.

"Alice, you take the dogs outside and give them a run before we head to the castle. Make sure they burn off any excess energy so they behave themselves."

"I'm on it. Come on, fluff balls." Alice took the dogs out and shut the door behind her.

I walked over to Gran and touched her shoulder. "You make a beautiful bride."

She turned, and I sucked in a breath as I saw tears in her eyes. "I'm not sure I can go through with this. What am I thinking, getting married at my age?"

"Gran! You can get married at any age. You and Ray are perfect for each other."

"Oh, I love the man, probably too much. But all this fuss. I should have had a ceremony in the local village hall and then a couple of drinks in the pub."

"Alice and Rupert wouldn't want you getting married anywhere else. This venue is perfect, and it's our home. It's only right you get married here. And the ceremony room looks stunning."

"It's too grand for me. I didn't grow up posh, and I shouldn't pretend now. I'm not sure I should have all of this."

"You deserve it." My gran had been through rough times, many of them partly her fault, after she stole from rich men. It was a revenge tactic after she got cheated out of her life savings by a lothario. But she'd served her time and was a reformed character, and she'd met the love of her life when she'd moved to Audley St. Mary. Ray was a kind, sweet man, and he was besotted with Gran, just as he should be.

Gran turned and looked out the window again. "It was generous of the Audleys to let me have the castle rooms for my wedding."

"It's their wedding gift to you and Ray. Ray's worked at Audley Castle for years, so they want to do right by him. And they like having you here, too."

"And all the flowers came from the gardens, and the catering is being done by Chef Heston ..."

"Don't forget, I made your wedding cake."

"And it'll be delicious." Gran smiled at me. "Oh, Holly! You look lovely in that dress. I suppose I shouldn't let everyone down by pulling out so late in the day."

"You love Ray, and he loves you. That's all that matters. Forget about everyone else and the swanky surroundings, just focus on that. That's what's important about today."

"What if ..." She went to chew on her nail.

I stopped her spoiling her manicure by catching hold of her hand. "Is something else worrying you?"

Gran's gaze dropped to the floor. "I don't want to let Ray down."

"Why would you do that?"

"He knows about my past. I'm far from perfect."

"None of us are perfect. But you're different now. And you've got Ray, Saffron, and me to keep you on the straight and narrow if you ever need a nudge in the right direction. The only way you'll let Ray down is if you don't get a wiggle on and get married to him."

"We should have gone to Las Vegas. We could have hopped on a plane, met an Elvis impersonator, and been done with it." She waved a hand at her fitted cream dress with its beautiful sparkling diamantes around the hem.

"And then you'd have missed seeing most of your friends and family who want to congratulate you. Plus, Saffron and Meatball would have hated to travel such a long way, and you wouldn't want them missing out. Did you see their bow ties?"

"I did. They're cute. And, no, I don't want them missing out. They're a part of our family."

"You deserve to be pampered. Enjoy the day."

She took a deep breath and squeezed my hand. "You're right. It's just my nerves."

"Of course. Now, is there anything you need before we leave?"

Gran puffed out a breath. "Remind me how to breathe again."

I carefully kissed her cheek, making sure not to disturb the light covering of pretty make-up on her face. I couldn't be more delighted that she was marrying Ray. They made each other so happy.

I picked up her bouquet and handed it to her. "It's time to go."

She nodded. "And once this is over, you can start thinking about getting married to Rupert. He's a catch. My granddaughter, not only is she royal, she's also marrying a lord!"

I smiled, still a little starry eyed over the fact Lord Rupert Audley had proposed to me. And I'd turned him down! Well, it had been a shock proposal. We'd barely been on a real date, and there he was, on his knee asking me to be with him forever.

But we'd been seriously dating for several months, and everything had been going amazingly well. And Rupert really wanted to get married. Secretly, so did I, but I refused to be rushed into such a huge decision. Change was scary, and I was a bit of a coward when it came to big upheaval. I liked a quiet, simple life, but it wouldn't be so simple once I married into the Audley family.

"One wedding at a time, Gran," I said.

"She's in here! This way, ladies."

I turned at the sound of an unfamiliar voice approaching the front door. It was pushed open, and three eager faces looked in at us.

They were all women in their mid-sixties and dressed in their finest wedding outfits.

The tallest woman, who looked remarkably like Gran, squealed and raced over, engulfing Gran in a hug.

"Daphne Chamberlain!" Gran hugged her back.

"Molly! You look amazing." Daphne stepped away and smiled at her.

"You would say that, since we're practically twins."

The other two women raced in and hugged Gran.

Gran was laughing as she took a step back. "Holly, I'd like you to meet three friends of mine. This is Pearl Duchovny, she'll be entertaining us tonight as the singer in the band."

Pearl was curvy, with a magnificent bosom strapped into a red corset dress, her black hair piled on top of her head. She swooped in to give me a kiss.

"This beauty must be your granddaughter," she said.

"That's right," Gran said. "I always had your picture with me and would show you off any time I could."

I grinned. "It's nice to meet you all."

"This is Daphne Chamberlain." Gran introduced me to the woman who'd rushed in first.

"It's a pleasure." Daphne smiled at me.

"And this is Jane Napoleon," Gran said.

I nodded a greeting at her. Jane seemed more formal than the other two. She had perfect posture, was thin, and wore a deep blue linen suit that was crumpled at the elbows.

"You all look familiar," I said, "but I can't place any of you. How do you know my gran?"

Pearl chuckled. "There's a story. Who's going to tell it?"

"We've no time for your long stories, Pearl," Jane said. "Molly's got her wedding to get to. Let's get a move on."

"You don't get to order us around anymore," Pearl said. "We're free women."

Jane's forehead wrinkled. "I never did. I was one of the good ones."

They all laughed, while I looked on in confusion. Why would Jane be ordering them about?

Gran's eyes widened. "Can you believe it? I'm getting married."

"Of course we can," Daphne said. "You always were the prettiest of the group."

Gran laughed again before looking at me. "You probably saw this lot when you visited me in prison. Daphne and Pearl were inmates, and Jane was a guard."

"I'm retired now," Jane said. "But I keep in touch with my ladies. And these three were unforgettable. They always kept me on my toes during my shifts."

"Wow! I didn't know you remained close with anyone from prison," I said to Gran.

"Why not? You make the best friendships on the inside," Pearl said. "You quickly learn who to trust, and who to avoid. I knew Molly was a good 'un the second we met."

"And we bonded because we look so alike and people kept mixing us up," Daphne said. "We pretended we were sisters. We fooled so many people."

"You always pretended, and people believed us," Gran said.

"I'm glad you could all make it," I said. "It should be a fun day."

"It won't be fun for anyone if we hold the bride up any longer," Jane said. "Her groom will think we've kidnapped her."

"Oh! You're right," Gran said. "Come on, ladies, off you go. I'll meet you at the ceremony."

There was a thud on the front door, making Saffron yip.

Daphne groaned. "That'll be Reggie. He was complaining about having to drive us the short distance here to see you."

"You're still dating Reggie Frasier?" Gran's nose wrinkled. "Haven't you gotten rid of him yet?"

"I've tried a couple of times, but he keeps coming back like a bad smell. I'd better calm him down or we'll end up walking back to the castle, and my heels forbid that." Daphne hurried over and opened the door.

A tall, stocky guy with dark hair wearing a black suit stood outside, a scowl on his stubbled face. "We're going to be late. You know I hate being late for things."

"The bride is in here, Reggie. You remember Molly? They can hardly start the wedding without her," Daphne said.

Reggie didn't acknowledge Gran. "If you're not all in the car in the next minute, I'm leaving without you." He turned and stomped away.

"He's as charming as ever," Gran said.

"Ignore him. We had a fight before coming here, and he threatened not to bring me." Daphne shook her head.

"You should find yourself someone new at the reception tonight," Pearl said. "Someone who can put a smile on your face. Weddings always make people romantic."

"As does all the free champagne," Gran said.

Daphne sighed. "It's complicated with Reggie. Come on, ladies, we've held up the bride long enough, and I'm not walking back to the la-de-da castle in these shoes."

There was another flurry of hugs and kisses before they dashed out the door.

I helped Gran touch up her make-up and smoothed down her hair. "You didn't tell me you were inviting anyone from the prison. We looked at your guest list a dozen times, and I don't remember seeing their names."

Gran's cheeks flushed. "I didn't want to say anything in case you objected, or were worried they might misbehave."

"I'd never object to you having your friends here, no matter how you got to know each other. From the sounds of it, you looked out for each other when you were inside."

"We did. They're the best girls, and even Jane came in handy now and again. She was one of the more flexible wardens. We had a laugh together, and after she retired, we kept in touch online. I thought she could represent the prison side of my family."

"I'm glad they're here. They seem to make you happy."

"They're entertaining, that's for sure. And Pearl can really belt out a tune. I knew she'd gone back to singing after she got out and had to have her entertain us at the reception. She's really good. She could have been on the West End stage if she'd kept on the right side of the law."

I caught hold of Gran's shoulders and gave her a gentle squeeze. "I'm happy they're here. Now, no last-minute worries you need to get off your chest before Ray makes an honest woman of you?"

"Seeing the girls has helped relax me. I'm ready."

I tucked her hand into my crooked elbow, called the dogs, and headed to the front door. "Then let's get you married."

Maple Glaze and Murder is available to buy in paperback or e-book format.
ISBN: 978-1-9163573-7-2

Here's one more treat. Enjoy this recipe for lovely lemon drizzle cake. Saffron and Meatball approved!

Recipe – Lovely Lemon Drizzle Cake

Prep time: 20 minutes **Cook time:** 40-60 minutes

Recipe can be made dairy and egg-free. Substitute milk for a plant/nut alternative, use dairy-free spread, and mix 3 tbsp flaxseed with 1 tbsp water to create one flax 'egg' as a binding agent (this recipe requires 12 tbsp flaxseed to substitute 4 eggs.)

INGREDIENTS
1 cup (200g) unsalted softened butter
1 cup (200g) sugar
4 eggs
1 ½ (200g) cups self-rising flour
Zest of 2 lemons
Juice of 1/2 lemon

For the drizzle:
Juice of 2 lemons
3/4 cup (150g) sugar

INSTRUCTIONS

1. Pre-heat the oven to 350F (175C)

2. Grease and line a 2-lb loaf tin.

3. Cream the butter and sugar.

4. Add the juice of 1/2 lemon and beat until pale and creamy.

5. Beat in 2 eggs.

6. Beat in 1 egg with a tbsp of flour.

7. Beat in the 4th egg with a tbsp of flour and the lemon zest.

8. Place batter into the tin and bake in the oven for between 40-60 minutes, until a toothpick comes out clean.

9. Leave in the tin to cool.

10. Prick the cooled cake all over with a skewer.

11. For the drizzle - mix the sugar with the juice of 2 lemons and pour over the cake.

12. Enjoy!

CPSIA information can be obtained
at www.ICGtesting.com
Printed in the USA
LVHW102204051222
734655LV00024B/633